And The Jukebox Played Their Song

A Broome Park Prefab Village Novel

(Fabrian Feel Good Books)

Pat Posner

Cover Illustration: David Young –
http://www.davidyoungillustration.co.uk

Typesetting and Design Fabrian Books –
fabrianbooks.com.

For Everyone Who Asked for a long Broome Park Prefab Village Book

Chapter One

It's a Lovely Day Tomorrow!
(Vera Lynn)

"I love the sound of the hooter at five o'clock on a Friday afternoon." After pulling the cover over her typewriter Polly felt around under the desk and finding her shoes, slipped them back on.

Jumping up, she smiled round at the three older women in the flour mill factory's office. "It seems to make a different noise, as if it's as happy as we are to be getting two days off."

"Polly Richards, anyone would think you didn't like your job," one of them commented, checking everywhere had been left tidy before indicating they could all leave.

"It's not that bad," Polly replied as they joined the throng of workers making eagerly for the factory gates. "But I'm always glad when the weekend's about to start. And this one seems to have taken a long time to get here."

"That's because tomorrow's a big day for your chap, Polly, and you want to see if it comes up roses. Waiting for something like that makes time drag."

*

Tomorrow night had been on her mind all week. But, thought Polly as she made her way along the streets of terraced houses towards home, it's not having seen Johnny since last Sunday that's made time drag most of all.

She'd been disappointed when Johnny asked her not to go and watch him and the *Skifflers* rehearsing in his uncle's cellar like she usually did most weekday evenings. She enjoyed listening to the skiffle band Jonny had formed with four of his friends. Better still, she liked Johnny walking her home afterwards.

But he'd held her close and explained she was too much of a distraction. "I need to concentrate on getting the songs perfect for Saturday. "If you're at our practice sessions..."

Stepping back a little Johnny had sung a couple of lines from his own skiffle version of a popular Kitty Kallen song: *"I want to cross the room and kiss your lips, to show you you're not forgot. You are mine and I am yours and that means such a lot."*

That had cheered her up a little. She said she'd go to the pictures with her best friend, Jean, one evening to see *Summer Madness* - she quite liked Rossano Brazzi - and Jean's parents had a television; she might go round there to watch *The Grove Family*.

"And," Johnny had said, "how about meeting me on the market Saturday morning to help me choose a shirt?"

For his practice sessions Johnny always wore a white t-shirt and jeans and Polly thought, with the sides of his dark hair swept back and a quiff on the top he looked just like the picture of James Dean she'd seen on the cover of *Picture Show* magazine.

But, although he'd do his hair that way, he'd decided he wanted a short-sleeved open-necked shirt to wear for the big occasion.

It would be a big occasion, too. Because if Johnny Jake and the Skifflers won the "Grand Skiffle

Contest" at the Locarno, that meant they'd get a whole week's engagement at the Hippodrome.

Polly gave a child-like skip of joy at the thought. Her mum thought the only music worth a dot was the sort they had on the wireless programme *Friday Night is Music Night* and singers like Jimmy Young, Dean Martin and Al Martino.

Actually, Johnny had a lovely voice for singing ballads and crooning. He could sing blues and jazz numbers as well. For now, though, he preferred skiffle – which he said had its roots in jazz and blues anyway.

But… Polly crossed her fingers for luck; Mum might feel differently about her having a boyfriend who played in a skiffle group if they got an engagement at the Hippodrome where stars like Ruby Murray, Eddie Calvert and Tommy Cooper appeared.

It would lead to more bookings. Johnny would be a star, too, and not "someone who wastes his time making a racket on an old washboard and blowing into a stoneware jug (one Polly had "borrowed" from her mum) or on a paper-covered comb".

Mind, if Johnny and his band started playing at popular venues, going to watch them might be a problem. Mum wouldn't object to her going to the talent show tomorrow but she wouldn't take too kindly to her going to the Hippodrome and places like that. Still, that was something to worry about nearer the time.

Right now she was home and it was Gran's day for visiting them. Polly gave a small sigh of satisfaction to see the front door of twenty-two

Curzon Street propped open. With any luck she'd be able to sneak through the hall and up to her room and stay there until someone called her down.

Her mum's mother was the only grandparent she and her sister had. They'd never known their dad's parents who'd died when Dad had been quite young. So Gran should be special really.

It wasn't that she disliked her, Polly told herself, feeling slightly ashamed. More like she'd never really got to know her. That's because when she and Sarah were little Gran had only visited on odd occasions and then, during the war, they hadn't seen her at all. It was only after the war Gran had started coming round once every week or so.

Watching Gran and listening to her could be quite amusing; she did and said everything so quickly. But, against that, the atmosphere always seemed a bit tense when she was here.

*

Standing in the hallway, Polly slipped off her shoes. She'd be in for it if she made dints in the lino. It was quite a relief to get them off as well; stiletto heels were such a new fashion she hadn't got used to wearing them yet.

After rubbing her aching ankles, she tiptoed towards the living room then hovered outside the partially closed door to see if she could tell from her mum's or gran's voice how things were going. It was Gran talking...

"Like I said last week when we first discussed it, you're doing the right thing, Ivy. Spending a bit of time breathing sea air will put your Walter right back on his feet. Won't do you no harm neither after making that long journey week in week out to visit him in the sanatorium.

"Then there's your travelling into Manchester five mornings to get to work. It must take you forty minutes or so to get there and another forty back. Plus the waiting for the trains."

Gran had sounded warmer than usual and, even though she didn't seem to approve of Mum working in Manchester; she actually appeared to be praising her for planning to "spend a bit of time breathing sea air".

So, when Dad's discharged from the sanatorium he and Mum are having a day out, thought Polly, as her gran's words sank in. I expect they'll be going to Llandudno where Mum used to take me and Sarah to "blow the cobwebs away".

A picture of herself and her sister putting pennies, halfpennies and farthings in an old *Pan Yan* pickle jar - they'd called the Llandudno jar - popped into her mind. She'd been eight and Sarah nine when the war ended and they'd started to save up for those day trips.

Dad had still been in the army so he'd only been with them if he'd been on leave. He'd really enjoyed those outings, though. He was sure to be looking forward to going there again, just him and Mum.

Polly nodded and guessed they'd be going on a Saturday because her mum didn't work then. Or perhaps they'd spend the whole weekend there...

Maybe it would coincide with the time Johnny and the Skifflers were at the Hippodrome (if they won the contest). There wouldn't be a problem about her going to see them on the Saturday night if her parents were away.

Any thought of going up to her bedroom forgotten, Polly edged a little closer to the door so she wouldn't miss anything her mum said. She had a quieter voice than Gran.

"It's Walter I'm thinking of, not myself. Staying on in the army, even after what he went through in the war, and then having to come out because of getting tuberculosis, that didn't seem fair."

Polly shivered as she recalled the day they'd been given the awful news. But after weeks and weeks in the sanatorium, Dad was recovering well and would soon be home.

"Just keep on thinking positive, that'll help Walter most of all." Gran still sounded warm and sympathetic.

Polly remembered how once when she was little she'd asked Gran what had happened to Grandad and Gran had told her that, like a lot of other fathers and husbands, he hadn't come home after the Great War.

Maybe that's why Gran's sympathising with Mum, she thought. Dad getting ill was down to the *last* war. Gran wouldn't want to think of Mum losing her dad and her husband because of wars - Dad's been really poorly, he could have died.

"I know we've not always seen eye to eye, Ivy," Gran was saying now, "but I'm glad you've let me work things out with you this last couple of weeks."

Polly knew her mum had been worried out of her mind. Talking to Gran had obviously helped. It was clear today wasn't the first time they'd discussed it though. Polly felt a bit hurt Mum hadn't said anything to her about this planned outing.

I suppose she was waiting until it was all fixed up, she told herself. I'll hear about it sooner or later so I might as well go up to my room now.

She had only taken a couple of steps when her mum's next words stopped her in her tracks.

"It will be a relief to get Polly away from that Johnny lad she's so keen on. Fair enough, he always walks her home, comes in sometimes, but I often wonder what the neighbours think when they see the way he dresses and does his hair. I really don't like her going around with him and his friends in their so-called skiffle band.

"It's a shame he'd already done his National Service before Polly met him. That would have kept them apart a couple of years. I'll just have to hope that three months apart will take her mind off him and put an end to it."

Three months apart? Polly searched anxiously for the meaning behind those words. And they could only mean one thing. Nobody had been talking about a day out in Llandudno - but about months of "breathing sea air".

And her mum was obviously planning on taking her with them. To keep her away from Johnny. Temper flaring, Polly strode into the room.

*

Sitting up in bed, Polly fumbled for the torch she kept on her bedside table. Switching it on, she cast its beam over the alarm clock. Three o'clock. Hadn't she heard somewhere it was at that hour in the morning a person could feel at their lowest ebb?

It was certainly true for her right now. Her earlier anger and indignation had died away and all she felt was… "Misery and helplessness," she murmured.

OK, so she hadn't wanted to go to Llandudno with Mum and Dad. But to be told they didn't want her with them, well, that had hurt. She'd have got over that quickly enough if they'd been leaving her here so she could carry on with her life.

That wasn't happening though, was it? Mum was packing her up and sending her off like an unwanted parcel. And the main reason for that, no matter what other reasons Mum had given, was to keep her away from Johnny.

Chapter Two

Too Young
(Nat King Cole)

"Won't she just let you stay in the house while they're away, Polly? Knowing that you were there, looking after it..." Johnny pushed away his empty plate and gazed at her from the opposite side of the café table.

They'd spent so long choosing him a shirt, and walking round all the market stalls looking for silver thimbles that would fit his fingers comfortably when he played his washboard, Johnny had been starving afterwards.

Thinking she'd be able to talk to him more easily when they were sitting down, Polly had agreed when he'd suggested coming here for something to eat. But she'd only ordered a *Pepsi* - she knew she'd not manage to get any food past the lump of misery in her throat.

Now, fighting back tears, she shook her head. She hadn't wanted to tell Johnny the awful news - not with the contest only hours away. But she'd had to explain why she wouldn't be at the Locarno tonight, watching him and the Skifflers.

"Mum says eighteen is too young to be trusted with that sort of responsibility. That's my sister's fault. Sarah was only just eighteen when she had to get married in a hurry."

Polly finished her drink before continuing, "Anyway, this friend of Mum's called Janice is renting our house for three months. Mum said she'll need that money to pay for the house she's taken in Llandudno.

"Janice is nice, I met her and one of her children once and I wouldn't have minded stopping in our house with her. But there'll be her husband and the other two children so there'd be no room for me as well."

"I could ask if you can come and stay at ours, Polly. We've got room and Mum thinks you're the cat's whiskers since you showed her how to make *Cheese Dreams*. She and Dad like you a lot. Think you're good for me for some reason," he added with a smile.

"Whereas my mother, for some reason, thinks the opposite about you. Oh, I know she's polite whenever you come in with me, but she isn't that keen on me going around with you so she'd probably have a seizure if I suggested staying at yours.

"She wouldn't even talk about me going to stay with Jean, or with our Sarah, either. It's no good, Johnny. It's all arranged and I'm to go and live at Gran's place while Mum and Dad are away."

Polly sighed. "I've never even been to Gran's and I can't remember Mum ever going, either, so I can't understand why she decided that."

"You've never been to your gran's?" Johnny looked surprised.

No wonder, either, thought Polly. Johnny had a large family and they all visited each other regularly. Johnny even worked for one of his uncles who owned a furniture wholesalers.

"I think there must have been some sort of falling-out between Mum and Gran at one time. Maybe Gran didn't approve of Mum's marriage or something. I always feel that Mum goes along with Gran visiting us only because it wouldn't be right to stop her from seeing me and Sarah. Not that Gran sees me for long. She always leaves about twenty minutes after I've got in from work."

"She probably needs to get home to make your grandad's meal."

"He died in the first world war. But my auntie Edna, Mum's sister, lives with Gran. Maybe it's Mum and Auntie Edna who had a falling-out. She was away doing her nurse training during the last war but when it ended she used to take me and Sarah out for the day sometimes."

Mum had come on some of those outings, though, and Polly could remember herself and Sarah feeling embarrassed when their mother and Auntie Edna got a fit of the giggles or tried to win a coconut at the fairground. They'd always seemed right good friends.

"I haven't seen Auntie Edna for a while. That's probably because she's a midwife now and works funny hours. She always sends me a nice birthday present with Gran though."

The presents weren't something practical but things to wear or use on special occasions - or a *Wade* figurine or a few copies of *Love Story Picture Library*. Maybe Mum hadn't liked Auntie Edna's choice.

"Haven't you ever asked your mum why you never go to your gran's place?"

"She always fobs me off by saying it's too far away and she suffers from travel sickness if she goes for a long journey on buses. But she takes a travel sick pill when she goes to visit Dad and she could do the same thing if we went to Gran's so that doesn't add up. It's a bit of a mystery, really."

"Well, she can't *make* you go there, Polly."

"Unless I run away from home she can make the rules until I'm twenty-one, can't she. And that's just what she's done. She's even written to the factory to explain the situation, told them why I wouldn't be working there anymore. She posted the letter yesterday morning before I knew anything about anything. I suppose they might take me back when I'm living at home again."

"So what will you live on while you're not working? It doesn't make sense at all."

"That's all been arranged, too. I feel like a blooming string puppet. Everyone's pulling my strings and I can't stop them. See, Auntie Edna's fiancé is an estate agent–"

"Her fiancé? Is she a lot younger than your mum then?"

"Not much, about six years I think. I suppose she is a bit old to be engaged and not married. P'raps she hasn't got married yet in case she had to give up work and didn't want to. Or maybe she lost her first love in the war. Anyway, her fiancé is giving me a temporary office girl job at the estate agent's. I'm to start on Wednesday. Ashton's it's called. Mum said Gran told her it's about a fifteen minute bus ride from her place."

"But why does all of that mean you can't come to the Locarno tonight? You're our lucky mascot, Polly."

"Oh, I nearly forgot." Polly opened her raffia basket-bag and rummaged through the necessary stuff she kept in in until she found the tiny washboard that had been part of the kitchen furniture in the dolls' house she'd had for her eighth birthday.

"I've brought this for you to have as your mascot because I can't be there," she said, passing it across the table.

"It's amazing, Polly. I'm sure it will bring good luck. It would be luckier still if you could be there as well."

"Tonight," she told him with a sigh, "I'm to stay in and help get our house ready for Janice and her family coming to live in it. I'm to pack whatever clothes I'll need for staying at Gran's as well. Jack, he's Auntie Edna's fiancé, has got a car and he's coming tomorrow morning to drive me there."

"Where did you say it is? You must know the address even if you've never actually been."

"Mum always addresses birthday and Christmas cards so I don't know the exact address. All I know is it's somewhere called Broome Park village.

"According to Gran, thc village was named after the park because the houses were built on some land that used to belong to it. Gran says it's a bit cut off from everywhere but it's nice because it's like living right out in the country. Well, that might be nice for her, but I'll go mad. And..."

Polly couldn't hold her tears back any longer. "It takes Gran over an hour-and-a-half to get home when she's been to see us. That means I'll hardly ever be able to see you because it's too far away. And that's just what Mum wants, I'm sure it is."

"Crikey. Please don't cry, Pippi," he said reaching across the table and gently pulling one of her hands away from her face.

It was Johnny's niece, Margaret, who'd first called her that when they'd looked after her one afternoon. She'd persuaded Polly to play hairdressers and she'd put Polly's hair into two sticky out pigtails. "Because you've got quite red hair," she'd told Polly.

Then, giggling, she'd shown Polly a book she'd been sent for her birthday. "See, I've made you look just like Pippi Longstocking."

Johnny had told Polly she looked cute and ever since then Pippi had become his pet name for her.

"Listen," he continued now, "I've been to Broome Park. I went last summer with Graham and Neville to listen to a jazz band play in an open air festival. That's where we first saw skiffle. It was performed during the band's break and we decided to start our own skiffle band. So, for me, that park is a lucky place and it isn't *that* far away from here. It might take a while on trains and buses but in a van–"

"What's the point in mentioning a van? Am I supposed to wave a magic wand so a van with a driver appears to drive me from Gran's to here whenever I want?"

"But I can drive and the Skifflers have got a van. At least, we will have by the end of next week. We've clubbed together and we're buying one from a friend who works in a garage. It's no good us just playing locally if we want to get known. With a van it'll be much easier and quicker to get to places out of the area."

Johnny smiled. "And," he added, "I'll be able to use it to come and see you. I won't be able to come Saturdays because I'm sure the Skifflers will be booked up for Saturday nights but I'll drive over some Sundays and one or two nights in the week as well. We can wander round my lucky park together."

"Really? Really, Johnny?"

He nodded. "But even if we hadn't been getting the van, I'd still have got to see you somehow. I wouldn't let a few miles keep me from seeing my girl."

"It's more than a few miles," Polly said, but her heart was singing with delight. Living at her gran's would be almost bearable as long as she'd still be able to see Johnny.

"I'll write to you tomorrow," she added. "You'll have the full address then and you can write back straight away to tell me about the contest."

"Then I'll write again when I get the van and let you know what day I'll be coming to see you. You won't have to wait too long, Pippi, I promise. And we can fix up times to telephone each other from telephone boxes as well."

*

They walked hand in hand to Polly's bus stop. Even though she knew, once Johnny had seen her onto the bus, it would be a couple of weeks before she'd be with him again – that was nothing to the three months it could have been.

And once he had use of the van, well, they'd likely go out for the whole day together on some Sundays. They'd hardly ever been able to do that before. Although she didn't like the idea of living in the country a day out in the country with Johnny would be so romantic.

Polly's euphoria lasted until she was waving goodbye through the bus window. Then she recalled what Mum had said to Gran: "It will be a relief to get Polly away from that Johnny".

Would that mean her gran wouldn't let her see him? Did Gran think eighteen was too young to be in love? *Could* she stop her from seeing Johnny?

No. Gran wouldn't be able to stop her from going places. Gran had her own life to lead. She won't put that on hold to stay in all the time and to make sure I do the same, Polly thought.

When I'm seeing Johnny on a week day night he could pick me up from somewhere near the estate agent's. I'll tell Gran I'd be late home because I'm going out with a friend straight from work and hope she doesn't ask who the friend is.

Polly couldn't think yet how she'd manage to spend a whole Sunday with Johnny, if her gran didn't want her to see him. She didn't really want to have to meet him in secret. But if there was no other choice, she'd find some way of doing just that.

*

Even though it seemed more than likely she'd still be seeing Johnny at least twice a week, Polly's indignation and resentment at being packed off like a parcel returned in full force as she walked along Curzon Street.

As usual on a sunny day, folk were sitting outside enjoying the weather - having a good gossip. And Polly soon realised, as more than one of them told her they'd miss her and they hoped she'd have a nice time at her grandmother's, that she was the main subject of interest.

Just think, this time yesterday she hadn't known she was going and now the whole blinking street seemed to have heard.

What made her crosser than anything was her next door neighbour saying: "I expect you're feeling one up on all of us, Polly, going off for a three month 'oliday. Your mum and dad to the seaside and you to your gran's.

"She were telling me last time we had a chat 'ow living where she do is like being in the country. Right lucky you are. You'll be hearing the cock crow and strolling through green fields like in that folk song like old Henry sings when we go on charabanc trips."

"Tell you what," Polly retorted. "You go to Gran's and stroll through green fields instead of me and I'll come and stop at yours."

"You could of stopped here with me, Polly. I did offer, but your mum didn't want to know."

Polly's temper didn't improve when, as soon as she stepped into the house, her mum said she'd expected her back earlier than this.

"We've got a lot to do, Polly. I want everywhere nice for Janice and her family and you've also got to sort out what you'll need to take with you to Gran's."

"You mean to the place I've never been to that's somewhere miles and miles away from here and my friends. I still think–"

"And *I* think that's enough, Polly. Just stop being so selfish. It's going to be an uphill task for me and your dad trying to get his health back. You're too young for a lot of things but you aren't too young to understand that."

"But–" Polly began. Her mum didn't give her chance to continue.

"In times like this we have to pull together, Polly. It'll be a help for me and your dad knowing you'll be with someone who'll keep a proper eye on you. I couldn't have expected your sister to do that. She's enough to cope with having a young baby to look after."

"I could have stayed with Jean or even next door. Mrs Baines would've kept a "proper eye" on me."

"They aren't family and your gran is. Besides, nice as Mrs Baines is, her main reason for offering was the thought of being paid to have you."

Her mum had a sort of beseeching look on her face when she added, "It won't be easy for your gran and Edna, suddenly having an extra person living with them."

"That's why–"

"Look, Polly. If they're willing to put up with you, then you should be willing to put up with them to help your dad get well again. Then you and Sarah can get to know him properly. Edna and I never had the chance of getting to know our dad. Count yourself lucky you've hope for that."

That hit home. Even though, what with him being in the army, she and Sarah had never seen that much of their dad, Polly did love him. Realising how selfish and unfeeling she'd been, she walked over and hugged her mum.

"Well, come on then," she said a couple of seconds later, "let's start sprucing this place up for your friend."

"Gran will be doing the same at hers, Polly. She'll have tied a scarf turban wise over her curls to stop her perm from frizzing and put on a cross-over pinny with a large pocket to put a bottle of *Windolene* and scrumpled newspaper in while she buzzes around like a blue-tailed fly getting your room ready for you."

Polly smiled reluctantly. It was an apt description; she'd often been amazed at how quickly Gran got from their house to the end of Curzon Street. She could just picture her dashing around her place with a feather duster.

Chapter Three

A Woman's Work is Never Done
(Traditional Ballad)

"Heavens, Peg," said Betty Jones as she walked into number five Broome Avenue's living room. "You've still got your pinny on. Don't tell me you haven't finished cleaning and tidying yet."

"Just been putting the finishing touches to it, Betty."

"It looked perfect when I called by this morning and it's almost tea time now. You always keep it nice but you seem to have gone an extra mile today."

Edna laughed. "Mum's gone overboard with Colgate's *Fab* - proving you can use it to wash anything and everything like it says in the advert. She's *Windolened* all the windows and mirrors and done every stick of furniture with silicone polish and elbow grease. She'd have polished the goldfish if she could of.

"The only time she stopped was when Rod Simmonds brought round that bed you've lent us, Betty. She had a glass of *Tizer* with him after he'd assembled it. I'll go and put the kettle on and she might have another sit-down and a cup of tea now you're here."

"I'm not sure *I'll* sit down." Betty waved a hand at the cushions. "The cushions are that plumped up I think I'd be scared to."

"Don't talk daft, Betty," Peggy said. "Just get over feeling scared and plonk yourself down. I am ready for a break and I don't intend craning my neck up to talk to you."

Peggy waited until her friend sat down then she sank gratefully into one of the armchairs. She felt more tired than she was prepared to admit. What with working at the cake shop yesterday morning and then going to Ivy's and staying a while longer than usual - because of that upset with Polly who'd been furious about coming to stay here - she'd been late home and late for going on her Friday night National Savings stamps round.

That meant she'd had to rush around everywhere, tearing off stamps and collecting money as quickly as possible, standing outside on doorsteps instead of going in for a bit of a chat. Even so, she'd been back much later than normal and by the time she'd had a bit of a snack and washed up it had been almost midnight before she'd got to bed.

She'd woken early and knowing she had a lot to do had got up and started in on things. And, like Edna had said, apart from having a glass of *Tizer* with Rod, she hadn't stopped.

As if she'd read Peggy's thoughts, Betty smiled across at her. "Worked like a Trojan, you have," she said.

"I just want it all to look nice for when Polly arrives. She's never been here before."

"That's down to our Ivy," Edna said as she pushed a tea trolley into the room. "There's no way to get here from hers just by train and she suffers dreadfully from travel sickness on long bus journeys so she couldn't bring Polly to see us. When Polly was younger, Ivy didn't want her coming here on her own. Mum and I have always gone to Ivy's or met up with them somewhere Ivy could get to without going too far on a bus."

Glad Edna had explained that, Peggy swallowed a small sigh of relief. Edna had been just fifteen when Ivy left home and had accepted that reason for her sister not visiting easily enough.

Oh, it was true that bus travel made Ivy really poorly, but there were pills that could help and Peggy often wondered if, over twenty years on, Edna thought it a good enough reason for Ivy never coming. It sounded like she did, though, and it had likely answered Betty's unasked question, too. Betty must have thought it strange Ivy and Polly never visited.

"It's a right shame that is, said Betty. "It must be awful having to avoid going on a bus. Still, even though her dad's health is the reason, it's nice your grand-daughter's coming here at last, Peg. I reckon, no matter what age they are, they count staying with their gran as something special."

"I do wish we had three bedrooms, though, Betty. I've thought that many a time when Edna's brought one or two kiddies to stay here overnight until a new brother or sister has been safely delivered."

Betty laughed. "That's happened a fair bit recently, hasn't it? Remember how Doreen Smith over the way thought you had six or seven kiddies living here because she saw different ones coming and going?"

"None of them stayed for a long time like Polly will be doing, so lack of privacy wasn't a problem then. I did have a word with Rod when he came about maybe putting a partition up in Edna's room. But–"

"Peg. Rod's a brickie not a carpenter." Betty shook her head. "Besides, I don't reckon it'd work trying to make one bedroom into two. It'd be like sleeping in a box and no room to swing a cat."

"That's what Rod said. Polly did share a bedroom with Sarah before Sarah got married but they're sisters and there's only a year's difference in age. I'm not sure how Polly will feel about having to share with her aunt."

"It was either that or share with you, Mum," said Edna, passing her a cup of tea. "And seeing how I'm often not here at night, what with babies hanging on until then to come into the world, it makes sense."

Peggy nodded and looked across at her friend. "I remember Edna telling me when she first became a midwife how the term midwife means with woman - meaning the woman with the mother assisting her with the birth. If you ask me, the mid part of it comes from middle of the night."

"You could be right, Mum," Edna agreed. "Whatever, Polly's likely to have the bedroom to herself more often than not."

"And she'll have a lovely bed, thanks to you lending me the one your daughter used to have, Betty. I'm really grateful for that," said Peggy.

"Wasn't doing any good just stood there unused most of the time. When my Mary and the grandkids come on a visit there's still one single bed in the second bedroom and the bed settee in the living room. We'll muddle in right enough. It's being together that counts."

Betty being so close to Mary was something Peggy secretly envied. Oh, she and Edna were close but she wished the same could be said about her and Ivy. They'd had a right good loving mother and daughter relationship until Ivy discovered the secret kept from her and Edna.

Peggy felt the usual regret filling her as unhappy memories crowded in. She really thought she'd done the best thing for all of them but Ivy hadn't been able to see it.

Ivy's words: "I'll never forgive you, Mother", lodged in Peggy's heart and still rang in her ears.

Thankfully, Ivy hadn't told Edna anything. That's when Ivy had left home though - saying she'd never come back again not even on a day visit. Oh, she hadn't completely cut herself off. She'd written regularly to her younger sister - and met up with her at times as well.

But when Ivy got married two years after she'd left, Peggy had known she'd only been invited to the wedding because Ivy didn't want to be thought in the wrong for keeping her mother away. Later, that had followed through on other special occasions, too - Sarah's christening and first birthday party and the same when Polly had been born…

Betty's laughter jerked Peggy out of her thoughts and she pulled herself back to here and now.

"It's the bedroom cupboard space you'll need to be firm on, Edna," Betty was saying. "If my grandkids are anything to go by, today's youngsters seem to have enough clothes to open a shop. Just make sure your niece leaves you room for you to hang up your things."

"Oh, I think I'll have enough room," Edna said. "Come and have a look at how we've arranged things, Betty."

Peggy watched them walk out of the room and her thoughts turned to the past again.

The war had started soon after Polly's second birthday. She hadn't seen much of Ivy and the little ones then, but after the war Ivy had agreed to her going there once a week to see Sarah and Polly. Not that she'd seen them for long, by that time they were at the age where they wanted to be playing out with their friends.

Then, when Sarah had started work, she was rarely home before I left, mused Peggy. And after Polly started at the flour mill, until she got home, it was just me and Ivy sat there together with the atmosphere all strained.

Mind, that had eased up a bit on her last two visits - though it hadn't been easy at first convincing Ivy that Polly coming to stop here was the best thing all round. But now it was happening.

Peggy smiled. It would be good to have this chance of getting to know her youngest granddaughter better. She'd lost all hope of that happening with Sarah now she was married and leading a new life.

But, Peggy told herself, if Polly and I could build a loving relationship it might help Ivy and me to become closer, too, and then Ivy might see her way to forgive what had happened in the past.

"So, how about it, Peg?" asked Betty. "Yes or no?"

"I don't think Mum even noticed we'd come back in, Betty, let alone heard your offer." Edna tapped Peggy's knee. "Anyone home?" she asked, laughing.

"Sorry, I was thinking of when Polly's here," Peggy replied. "How about what, Betty?"

"I asked if you fancied coming round to mine for a bite to eat," said Betty. "It'll just be us two. My Tom's got an away darts match. You've worked so hard, Peg. Edna told me this morning she's going out with Jack for a meal and I thought you might not feel like making one just for yourself."

"Thanks, Betty, love, that'll be really nice," Peggy replied, thinking how lucky she was having such a good friend. They'd known each other for six years now. Hit it off straight away the two of them had – back in 1949 when Peggy had seen Betty and her family moving in on the wettest day of the year and had lent them two big brollies and stayed to help Betty unpack.

They'd chatted about favourite food and moaned about how hard it was to bake a decent cake with most of the ingredients needed still being on ration. Peggy chuckled as she recalled how the following day, using artistic skill she'd made an ersatz Battenburg cake to welcome them to the village.

"It was one of my mornings for working at the cake shop yesterday," she said, "and I brought a Battenburg home. I'll bring that with me."

"Should be called a friendship cake really, Peg," Betty said. She obviously remembered the first Battenburg they'd shared, too.

"Talking of friendship, Betty, I'm hoping Polly will be able to find a few in the village she can come friendly with. What with the Simmonds' moving next door to you, Betty, their garden backs onto ours now and Polly's sure to see Rod of an evening when he's working in the garden. With any luck the two of them might get chatting."

"Peg, you're not trying to match-make even before the lass arrives? But if you are, what's wrong with Tony from next door? Didn't you say your Polly's eighteen? I'd of thought Tony's nearer her age than Rod."

"Tony's a nice enough young lad, thin as string, bless him, but he's awfully quiet and shy. Rod's only a couple or so years older than Tony. Strong-looking, too. Someone like him might help take Polly's mind off the skiffle playing lad she's been seeing. Ivy's hoping Polly being here away from him will put an end to it."

"I'm not so sure about that, Mum," said Edna. "It could be the real thing. It was for me and Robert and I was her age when I started seeing him. If he hadn't got killed in the war, I reckon we'd still have felt the same way even after being apart."

"Oh, well, time will tell," Peggy said. "There isn't only Rod. I'll take her with me on my National Savings stamps round. There's more than one family with lads and lasses around Polly's age. She might get friendly with some of them."

"Jack told me there's a coffee bar opening a few doors down from the estate agency," said Edna. "That will be a good place for Polly to go of a lunch time. There's sure to be others her age there. So she'll have plenty of opportunity to make new friends."

Edna shrugged. "Don't forget the old saying, though: "Absence makes the heart grow fonder". It could easily work out that way for our Polly and her skiffle playing lad."

Chapter Four

Unchained Melody
(Jimmy Young)

"Are you all right, Polly?" Jack glanced at her briefly then turned his attention back to the road.

He'd arrived to take her to her gran's at quarter-past ten. They'd been travelling for well over an hour now, and after a bit of chat about the car (Jack told her it was an Austin A30), the weather (sunny and warm) and the television programme *The Grove Family* (Polly had only seen it once when she'd watched it at her friend Jean's house last week), a silence had fallen.

Perhaps that was because Jack had a sort of serious, solemn manner about him. And, although he was Auntie Edna's fiancé, which made him almost an uncle, he was also the proprietor of Ashton's Estate Agency and soon to be her boss. Polly supposed she should make an effort to start up another conversation.

To be truthful, she wasn't sure how to address him. When he'd arrived this morning he'd introduced himself as Jack but maybe she should call him Mr Ashton? She sensed him glancing at her again and tried to work out an answer to his question.

Was she all right?

"I just feel a bit...a bit..." she began. Well, how did she feel exactly? Strangely, not too miserable.

Not yet at any rate. That was down to the letter (more of a note, really) from Johnny. It was the first thing she'd seen when she'd gone downstairs.

He must have pushed it through the letterbox in the early hours and it had been waiting for her on the doormat. She'd unfolded the sheet of paper quickly and read the few sentences scrawled on it: *The tiny washboard mascot worked, Pippi. We won the contest. I'll see you soon. If I could send you a song it would be Unchained Melody.*

She was wearing her full-skirted yellow dress and had put Johnny's note into one of its big pockets. Now, she slipped her hand into that pocket and, closing her eyes, touched the paper.

Only a short note but it was like a love letter. The first one she'd ever had. Mentioning *Unchained Melody* meant Johnny thought of her as his love, his darling and needed her love. And what were the rest of the words to the song?

"You feel a bit what, Polly?" Jack's anxious-sounding question interrupted her thoughts. "The car isn't making you poorly, is it? Are you like your mum? Edna told me she isn't a good traveller. Wind your window down and get a bit of fresh air and there are some barley sugar sweets in the glove compartment. Sucking one might help."

Polly opened the window but refused a barley sugar. "It's all right. I'm fine, thanks. I don't get travel sick. But I suppose I'm..."

"A bit nervous, I expect. There's no need. Your gran is so looking forward to having you there. Edna is as well. She was hoping to come with me to fetch you but she had to go and see one of her new mums."

"I haven't see Auntie Edna for a while. I think the last time was on my fourteenth birthday. We went to a fair and Mum came as well. I can remember her getting cross because Auntie Edna took me on the Waltzers twice on a trot and I felt poorly when we got off. Gosh, I haven't thought about that birthday for ages."

Polly giggled. "Auntie Edna won a goldfish as well - on the shooting range - but Mum wouldn't let me have it, said it didn't look like it had long for this world and she didn't want me and our Sarah crying for days like we did when our tortoise died. So Auntie Edna took it home with her."

"That must be Midas. Edna told me she won him at a fair."

"You mean she's still got him?"

Jack nodded. "In a very large goldfish bowl that sits on the sideboard in the living room. That will give you something to talk about if you're a bit nervous at first."

"I don't think I will be," Polly told him. "It will be strange, though, seeing as I've never been to Gran's before and now I'm going to be living there for months. Strange starting a new job in your estate agency as well," she added.

"There's no need to feel anxious about that, either. Edna told me you'd done office work since you left school. You'll pick everything up in no time."

"Gran told Mum it's a fifteen minute bus ride away," Polly said. "But if Gran's is a bit cut off from everywhere, I suppose it'll be quite a walk to the bus stop."

"Look." Jack pointed. "That's where you'll catch the bus."

Polly noticed a red pillar box, too. She'd be able to post her letters to Johnny on her way to work. Though she hoped there'd be a pillar box close to her gran's for the letter she wanted to write and post later today.

"In a few minutes," Jack continued, "we'll be turning into Blakeley Road which is the start of Broome Park village. I'll drive slowly once we've turned off so you can get a bit of a feel for the place."

"Does Ashton's have houses to rent or for sale there, Jack…erm, sorry…Mr Ashton?"

"Oh, Polly, I should have realised you might feel awkward about that side of it. We're almost family so Jack is fine when we aren't at work. But it will probably be best to call me Mr Ashton at work."

He smiled then went on, "To answer your question, the homes in Broome Park village are council-owned so Ashton's doesn't handle them at all.

"We've a couple of properties along this stretch of road coming onto our books, though. You'll probably be typing up the details of them, Polly. Now, just up ahead, look, is the signpost pointing to Broome Park village."

Polly nodded, thinking that it would be more than just a bit of a walk to the bus stop every morning.

"Right, so this is Blakeley Road," Jack said, turning into it. "The park the village is named after is over there," he added, pointing. "And Peg lives on Broome Avenue, which is off this road, about half-way down on the right."

For the briefest of moments the main thing Polly noticed were the front gardens full of flowers and flowering bushes - and the heady perfume from them that floated through the open car window. Then, immediately, she realised something else.

"But they don't look like houses, Jack. They remind me of those camping coaches converted from corridor railway carriages, or large beach huts, though camping coaches and beach huts don't have flat roofs and all these places have."

Jack slowed to a halt and turned to face her. "They're prefabs, Polly. Short for prefabricated buildings. You'd have been, what, around nine when the war ended? Probably too young to realise what a massive shortage of housing there was.

"The government decided factories that had previously made aircraft, tanks and suchlike, should make homes that could be transported in sections to ready prepared sites. Once they arrived on site, they were put up and ready to move into within days."

"Must have been like building a large scale version of a *Bayko* model house," said Polly, remembering how she'd once made a *Bayko* house with Johnny's niece. "Only the models looked more like proper houses than these prefabs do," she added, looking from one side of the road to the other.

"I believe there are some two storey ones in other areas," said Jack. "These are more like bungalows."

Polly put her head out of the window. Someone in one of the prefabs had a wireless on because she heard the signature tune of *Two-Way Family Favourites*. She had a sudden image of herself and Sarah as little girls during the war sitting with Mum listening to it; it had been called something different then but she couldn't remember what.

All these years later, Mum still switched the wireless on at twelve noon on Sundays. No good thinking of that, though, else she'd be admitting she was already homesick.

There were a few people walking along Blakeley Road - children of all ages and adults, too. They all looked smart and Polly guessed they were coming home from church.

She watched a man, a woman pushing a pram, two boys and a girl walking up the garden path and going in through the prefab's front door. "If they all live there, it must be quite a squash for them," she said, turning to look at Jack. "You said Gran's place is in an avenue off this road. Are the houses there proper ones?"

"All the homes in Broome Park village are single storey prefabs," Jack replied as he started the car again. "Wait until you see inside Peg's, Polly. I think you'll be surprised at how much room there is."

Polly sighed and leaned back against the car seat. Oh, the gardens and the surrounding area were nice enough if you liked the almost being in the country feeling (personally she preferred the cobbled streets and the terraced house with front doors opening right onto the pavement).

She really didn't like the idea of living in one of these shed-like buildings even if it was for only three months.

Chapter Five

Accentuate the Positive
(Bing Crosby/Andrews Sisters)

"Here we are, Polly. And your gran's waiting at the gate to welcome you."

"I didn't know she had a dog." Polly gazed at the long-haired black and white collie sitting at her gran's side. "Mum once told me she vaguely remembered having one when she was little."

"That's Laddie," Jack said. "He isn't Peg's. He lives next door. He thinks Peg's the bees' knees, though, and the feeling's mutual." Jack got out, walked round the car to the passenger side and opened the door.

"Come on, Polly. I'll see to your luggage. Laddie won't bite you. Nor will Peg," he added with a smile.

He's really nice, is Jack, thought Polly, realising he understood that she suddenly felt shy and uncertain. Then, taking a deep breath, she got out and walked towards Gran and her four-legged companion.

Laddie stood up and, tail wagging, gazed at Polly with gentle brown eyes. Relieved at the chance of delaying speaking to her gran, she concentrated on the dog instead. "Hello, you handsome fellow," she said, letting him sniff her hand before she stroked him.

"You're honoured, Polly love. Laddie usually acts a bit stand-offish before he makes friends with someone. Mind, I told him as soon as the car pulled up that you're my grand-daughter come to stay a while so happen he understands you're family and wants to make you feel welcome. Same as Edna and I do."

Polly looked up and, from the expression on her gran's face, guessed that she felt uptight about this as well. It's silly really, Polly told herself. It wouldn't have been like this if I'd been coming here since I was tiny – the way it happens in most families. And it isn't Gran's fault or mine I've never been before.

For a moment, Polly felt angry with her mum for never bringing her here – then annoyed with herself for not asking if she could visit on her own. She'd been old enough to do that for the last few years, hadn't she!

"We really do want you to feel welcome," her gran said, and Polly realised she'd been frowning.

"That's good to know." And Polly, seeing the worried lines on her gran's face relax, stepped round Laddie and gave her a quick hug.

"Eeh, Polly, love, you've not done that since you were knee high to a ladybird."

Polly laughed at the image that conjured up and was surprised at how pretty Gran looked when she joined in the laughter.

"It's good to see you sharing a joke," Jack said. "But are you going to stand outside much longer, Peg? These cases of Polly's are starting to feel like they're full of cement."

"Sorry, Jack," she replied. "Don't know what I'm thinking of. Even Laddie's got fed up and is going back next door." Then, still chuckling, she linked a hand through Polly's arm and led the way up the garden path and inside.

As her gran pointed to the doorways leading off the small hallway, saying, "Bathroom, a separate indoor toilet, the living room overlooks the back garden, the kitchen is off the living room, my bedroom's the back one and you'll be sharing the front bedroom with your auntie Edna, we've done a bit of reorganising and shuffling around to give you as much space as possible," Polly's stomach rumbled.

"Is that roast chicken I can smell, Gran?"

"Your mum said it's your favourite, Polly. We do have a small roast most Sundays. Usually belly pork or stuffed breast of lamb. But today's special so it's chicken. It'll be ready in an hour or so. Edna should be back from visiting one of her new mums long before then.

"You'll be staying of course, Jack," she added, turning from Polly to look at him.

"Try stopping me, Peg." Jack laughed and pointed at the cases he'd put down on the floor. "Where are these to go?"

"Shall we just pop them inside the bedroom door for now, Polly, while I show you around?" Polly didn't have time to comment before her gran had suited action to words.

"Not that it will take long," Gran continued, closing the bedroom door. "But all the rooms are a fair size even though there aren't many of them."

"While you're doing that, Peg," Jack said, "I'll go down to The Woodman's for a quick half unless you need me for anything?"

"No, but make sure it is a quick one, Jack."

"Right. I'll only be twenty minutes."

"You could bring some bottles of *Babycham* back.

Go down well with our chicken, they will and we can drink a proper toast to you," she added, smiling at Polly.

Polly decided that however tiny and cramped she found the place, she'd do her best to hide it and, as in the song her mum liked so much - she'd latch on to the good things because Gran was obviously saying and doing all she could to make her feel welcome.

Fancy cooking a chicken dinner. For most folk that usually only happened at Easter or Christmas. Her stomach rumbled again at the thought as she was guided into the living room.

"We have our main meal in here, Polly." Her gran waved a hand towards the dining table with four oak chairs tucked in underneath it. "It's nice looking out over the back garden while we're eating. For breakfast and other times we pull down the ironing board in the kitchen and use it as a table."

Polly nodded and walked over to the sideboard, laughing when she saw Midas swimming happily in and out of the greenery in the large bowl. "Jack told me Auntie Edna's still got the goldfish she won at the fair."

Then, turning, she glanced around the room: as well as a two-seater settee there were two comfy-looking armchairs either side of the fireplace and the fire with glass doors, a pretty rag rug in front of the fireplace and a bookcase in the alcove.

Wandering over to look at the books, Polly noticed quite a few of them were children's books. There was a small pile of comics, too.

"Those are for when Edna brings little ones here if

there's no-one to keep an eye to them while their mum's giving birth. Mind, I think Edna has a little read of them now and then as well."

"I've still got some *Sunny Stories* magazines from when I was little," said Polly. "I often flick through them and laugh at the pictures of naughty goblins or pretty fairies with magic wands."

"Your mum and Edna both loved pixies and elves and fairy tales when they were little. Oh, and Rupert Bear in the Daily Express. We often made up our own stories and drew pictures to go with them."

"Mum's never told me that, Gran."

"Your mum's drawings weren't up to much, nor were mine. But your auntie Edna's were really good. We used to call her Miss Mary after her who drew Rupert. You know, I've still got a lot of those pictures. Packed away in a big old leather satchel, they are. I'll have to rootle them out one day. Eeh, Polly, I haven't thought about those times for years. But come on now, I'll show you the rest of the place."

After a look at the kitchen which, to Polly's amazement had a fridge, and then the bathroom and separate toilet and a quick peek into Gran's bedroom, Polly was ushered into the bedroom she was to share with her aunt.

"This is your bed," her gran said, picking up Polly's cases and putting them on it. "Edna's made space for you to use in the wardrobe and emptied two drawers. When you've finished unpacking you can put your cases under the bed."

"Thank you, Gran. It's a nice bedroom."

"I'll leave you to settle in and I'll go and listen to the wireless while I'm seeing to the cabbage and carrots. Fresh picked this morning the veggies were, from my friends Tom and Betty Jones's garden.

"They live just round the corner on Blakeley Road, Polly. Betty will likely be popping in later to meet you."

*

It felt a bit strange with the bedroom being downstairs - or, make that on the same level as all the other rooms because of course there weren't any stairs. But even with two single beds - and a cabinet in between - a dressing table and a built in wardrobe, the bedroom didn't seem at all cramped.

The beds were quite high off the floor and covered with pretty chenille bedspreads - both white with a raised floral design and fringed edges.

Gran's right, thought Polly, shifting her cases a little so she could sit on her bed. All the rooms are a good size. The big windows make them light and airy but everywhere feels cosy and homely as well.

There was a small pile of books on the bedside cabinet and Polly was delighted to see they were all romance novels. That was another good thing to latch on to. If Auntie Edna liked reading romances (as well as comics and children's books) then maybe she'd understand about Johnny.

This time yesterday, Polly mused, I was with him. Sighing, she took the note out of her pocket. "It seems like ages ago now. I'm missing you already," she murmured, running a finger over the few lines he'd written.

Vaguely aware of Jean Metcalfe's voice, Polly guess Gran had tuned into *Two-way Family Favourites.*

It was quite an eerie experience when the requested song started and it turned out to be *Unchained Melody*. Polly quickly opened one of her cases and pulled out her old teddy bear. She'd brought Wilbert with her to cuddle at times like this.

Chapter Six

Getting to Know You
(Dinah Shore)

"From the expression on your face I'd guess this song is special in some way. Or is it the singer you like?"

Startled, Polly opened her eyes to see her aunt smiling down at her.

"I didn't hear you coming in, Auntie Edna."

"You were too busy dreaming. But hello and welcome, Polly."

"Hello. Long time no see," Polly replied. Then she wished she hadn't said that. Her mum really disliked her using that phrase.

Auntie Edna didn't seem to mind it though because she nodded. "Yes, it's been far too long. Stand up and let me get a proper look at you. And maybe we can drop the Auntie. It makes me feel old."

Even though she's wearing her uniform - which is far from being fashionable - she looks attractive and quite young, Polly thought as she put Wilbert down and got to her feet.

The note from Johnny fluttered to the floor. Polly bent quickly to pick it up. Then she folded it carefully before putting it back in her pocket.

"You've got that dreamy look on your face again, Polly. Is that a love letter? I asked you if Unchained Melody was your special song, well mine and Jack's is one by Dick Haymes called *Love Letters Straight from the Heart.*

"Jack sent me the record a while back when he was away on a training course and we couldn't see each other for what seemed like ages. I'll play you it sometime if you like."

Even though she must have been years older than I am when Jack sent her that record, she really will understand how I feel about being parted from Johnny, thought Polly.

"I'd love to hear it, Edna," she said. "I often have an evening playing records. Not that I've got many. I drive Mum mad sometimes playing the same ones over and over."

"I've got quite a collection." Edna lowered her voice. "I often drive your gran mad, too, when I settle down for an evening of listening to them. I like jazz and blues and your gran's not keen on that sort of music. She's more for ballads and romantic songs. I like them as well, though. So does Jack. We like all sorts of music really. If I'm not working on a Friday evening Jack comes round and we listen to *Friday Night is Music Night*."

"Do you like skiffle?" Polly asked.

"What little I've heard, yes. There was a jazz band in Broome Park last summer and they put on a skiffle set as part of their performance."

Polly gasped. That must be the same band Johnny went to see. Just think, he could have stood right next to Edna. She was about to say something about it but Edna was talking again:

"And for my birthday in October, Jack took me to a jazz concert at the Free Trade Hall in Manchester. Lonnie Donegan was in one of the bands and he did a couple of skiffle numbers. I think they're on one of my LP records."

"I don't remember seeing a gramophone or records in the living room," Polly said. "I'm sure I'd have noticed."

Edna laughed. "I've got a portable record player. Your gran wouldn't like it cluttering the place up so I keep it and my boxes and racks of records under my bed. You can have a good look and play whatever records you like, Polly. But best leave it until morning when your gran's at work."

Polly knelt down, lifted the fringed edge of the bedspread and had a quick peek under Edna's bed. "Gosh, it looks like you've loads of records. I'll look forward to going through them," she added, getting back to her feet and straightening her dress.

"I love that dress, Polly. Yellow suits you. We'll have to have your bridesmaid's dress made in that colour I think."

"Bridesmaid's dress?"

Edna nodded. "Oh, I know I haven't asked you yet, I should have because there's only two months to go now, but you will be one of my bridesmaids, won't you? I'm asking Sarah, too. My friend Gwen is my chief bridesmaid and we're having Jack's little nieces for flower girls."

"You mean you're having a big, white wedding?"

"Maybe not big. But yes, it will be a white wedding. I suppose you think I'm too old for that, Polly, and for going to jazz concerts and for having a special song?"

"No, I think it's all really romantic and I'd love to be one of your bridesmaids."

"When I throw my bouquet, I'll make sure I throw

it in your direction. Right now, I'd better get washed and changed."

"And I'll start unpacking," said Polly. She pointed to the old teddy, "Wilbert is the only thing I've unpacked so far."

Edna hurried out and Polly smiled. Edna clearly took after Gran when it came to talking and moving quickly. But surely she couldn't have got her romantic streak from Gran? Maybe she had, though. After all, Gran must have still been quite young when she was widowed and she'd never remarried. That could be because Gran believed that true love only happened once.

Whatever, seeing as her aunt was so much into music and going to see bands, it looked more and more as if she would be a good ally.

"She'll probably think it's quite something me having a skiffle-playing boyfriend, Wilbert," Polly told the bear as she opened one of her cases. "I might tell her about Johnny next time we're alone together."

*

"Do you want me to do anything, Mum?" asked Edna, walking into the kitchen.

"There's some chicken fat ready in that roasting tin, Edna, and I'll drain the veg and put them in dishes so you can have the liquid off them. Jack should be back any time so you can make the gravy," Peggy replied, thinking how bonny her daughter looked in her summery polka-dot dress.

By, when Edna got married, she'd miss her so much. Still, Polly would still be here for a month or so after that. Hopefully, she'd know her grand-daughter much better by then.

"Sounded like you and Polly were getting on like a house on fire, Edna. She wasn't half as chatty with me," she added, trying to hide a spurt of almost jealousy. "What were you talking about?"

Edna smiled as she opened a cupboard and took out the *Bisto* gravy powder. "Songs, song titles, singers and different sorts of music mainly."

"Happen I'll try and bring that sort of thing into a conversation with her. It might get her talking more natural to me then. Did she mention skiffle and that lad she won't be seeing while she's staying here?"

"She asked me if I liked skiffle," Edna replied as she poured some of the water from the vegetables onto the gravy powder and started to stir it. "She didn't say anything about her boyfriend but I'm sure she'd been thinking about him.

"I don't see how you can stop her from seeing him you know, Mum. You can't keep her locked up."

"Don't talk silly, Edna. I've no intention of doing anything like that. I wouldn't want her having him here, though. Leastways, not if neither of us were in. But I won't be telling her she can't see him. Though I reckon that's what Ivy were hoping I'd do. No, it'll be the effort of him getting here or our Polly getting there that'll keep them apart. Ivy said he hasn't got a car and, as I know from experience, it takes a while on public transport."

"When you're in love having to travel a couple of hours to be together won't matter. And if they're truly in love, they'll work something out.

"Talking of love," Edna smiled and a blush spread over her cheeks, "I heard Jack's car then. You finish the gravy, Mum, and I'll go out and greet him.

"Oh, and I'll try and think of a way to give you and Polly the chance of a cosy chat this afternoon so you can get to know each other a bit better," she added before dashing off.

Happen the chicken dinner and a glass of *Babycham* will make Polly feel more at ease with me, Peggy thought. And I'd best call her and ask her to go and sit at the table.

Chapter Seven

When You've Got Friends and Neighbours...
(Billy Cotton & his Band)

"That was the best chicken dinner I've ever had, Gran," Polly said when they'd finished eating.

She'd enjoyed the party atmosphere with them all sitting round the table chatting, eating and laughing - and Jack holding up his glass and making a toast to her. Jack had really lost his serious air over the meal.

"Mum's a dab hand with chicken dishes, Polly," Edna said. "Just wait 'til you taste her *Coronation Chicken*. She's making that for our wedding reception," she added, smiling lovingly at Jack.

"Ideas above her station, has Edna," Gran laughed. "Thinks she'll become royalty when she married Jack instead of just becoming Mrs Ashton."

"Royalty or not, Jack can get in practice for married life right now and help me with the washing-up," said Edna. "You and Polly could go and sit in the garden, Mum, and you can tell her where everything is round here and who lives where."

"That's a good idea, isn't it, Polly love?" said her gran. "I'll go and get my knitting. I might get the sleeves of my jumper finished while we're talking."

"I'll go and put some sun cream on," said Polly.

Jack jumped to his feet. "I'll fetch the deckchairs and put them up for you, Peg."

Eager to get us out of the way so he and Edna can be alone, thought Polly as she walked towards the bedroom. It's quite sweet really. But she'd been going to offer to help clear away and wash-up and she'd planned, after that, to sit on her bed and write to Johnny.

Sighing, Polly smothered her face and arms with *Astral.* At least she had a genuine excuse she'd be able to use for not staying in the garden too long and it would be good to find out about the area.

She hoped it wouldn't come to it, but if Gran did try to stop her seeing Johnny she'd need to know of a place near here where they could meet when he drove over to see her. Somewhere Gran wouldn't see her getting into his van.

*

Her gran was already in the garden when Polly went out. And, Polly noticed with a smile, Laddie was here, too, stretched out over Gran's feet.

Jack had put the deckchairs in a shaded part but Polly still planned to use the excuse of not being able to sit in the sun too long. (It was true, and everyone knew those with hair her colour, and the pale complexion that went with it, burnt easily and even though it was early September the sun was hot.)

She'd make sure to ask where the nearest pillar box was. And what time the last collection was on a Sunday. Then, after fifteen minutes or so, she'd go back inside to write her letter and, if the pillar box wasn't too far away, there'd be time to catch the post.

Having worked things out to her satisfaction, she murmured a greeting to Laddie - got a tail wag in response - and lowered herself onto the deckchair.

"Right, love," said Gran, as she started knitting so fast that watching her made Polly dizzy. "I'll start the guided tour. This is number five. As you know Laddie here is from next door. The numbers here aren't odds one side, evens the other. They go sort of circular.

"So Laddie's from number six. He belongs to Jenny and Ron Pearce. Jenny's laid up right now with a broken ankle so I've been walking Laddie in the afternoons. They've a daughter, Rita, who's the same age as you. She's working away for the summer, though. And then there's Tony who's a year older. Nice lass and lad, they are. Tony's got a good job at the Town Hall."

Oh, heck, thought Polly. I hope Gran isn't thinking of doing a bit of match-making to try and take my mind of Johnny. Mum told her she hoped me being here would do that.

"Doubt you'll see anything of Tony, though," her gran added, much to Polly's relief. "Right quiet and shy, he is. You'll have noticed Broome Avenue is a cul-de-sac?"

Polly nodded.

"Set back from where the road curves, there's a stile you can go over to get into Broome Park."

Sounds promising, thought Polly. I could go over the stile and walk to the furthest away entrance to meet Johnny.

"The four prefabs opposite ours and next door's back onto the park," her gran continued. "There's no-one your age over the way, though. Flo and Connie who live at number three are older than me. The other families over there all have three or four young kiddies. The Claytons, who live at number four, the other side of the stile, keep hens and a cockerel as well. Likely he'll wake you up early of a morning with his crowing."

"Crikey." Polly spoke without thinking. "Mrs Baines, her from next door back home, said how me coming here would be like in the folk song where they stroll in green fields and hear the cock crow. Sound like she were flipping well right."

Gran knitted faster than ever. "Never did like that neighbour of yours over much. There's plain nosiness and then there's neighbourly interest and folk you can tell something in confidence and know it would be safe. It's proper caring friendliness we have here in the village. Take your bed for instance. My friend, Betty Jones, the one I mentioned before, lent us that."

Polly nodded. "Betty's the one who lives on Blakeley Road."

"That's right, love. Number twenty. "Betty and Tom's next-door neighbours, the Simmondses, that's their garden backing onto ours, they've got two sons and the eldest one, Rod carried the bed round. Got good muscles like that Reg Park who won Mr Universe a couple of years back, or Charles Atlas in those adverts in the back of comics, has Rod."

Gran glanced up from her knitting and smiled. "He's in his early twenties, right good-looking an' all, Polly. You'll likely see him doing a bit of gardening of an evening when he gets in from work. That'll make a few in the village envious. All the lasses, the young and not so young, carry a torch for Rod."

I expect Gran reckons she's been crafty mentioning lots of other neighbours and making them sound uninteresting or too young or old for me to become friendly with and then telling me about a good-looking lad with muscles, thought Polly.

"Well, don't expect me to swoon," she said. "I can't stand men who think having big muscles make them the be all end all." Realising she'd been rude, she apologised. "Sorry, Gran. That didn't sound very nice."

"Rod isn't a show-off, Polly. He's a really nice young man. Doesn't seem to have a girlfriend though, so maybe he's waiting for the right one to–"

But before Gran could say any more, the slightly tense atmosphere was broken by the sound of singing from the kitchen.

"That's a jazz song," said Polly. "A friend of mine's got it on a Barbara Thomas record a cousin in South Africa sent. It's called *Pickin' a Chicken*. That must be what Edna and Jack are doing," she added, laughing. "Picking the chicken."

Laddie jumped up and pawed at Polly's knee.

"He recognised the last word," said Gran. "I saved a few slices for tomorrow, to go with a salad. You pop in and fetch Laddie a piece out, Polly. He knows not to go inside ours when Edna's there. She's all right out in the open air but she's a bit allergic to dog hair and gets wheezy if she's close to a dog indoors."

"Mum told me she remembered having a dog when she was very young," said Polly. "Is that when you found out about Edna being allergic to dog hair?"

"No, Edna wasn't born when we had Scamp." Gran's fingers slowed on her knitting and she took a deep breath. "We...I... 1917 it was when I said goodbye to Scamp. Lovely dog he was, bit like Laddie, here."

Looks like talking about Scamp really upsets Gran, Polly thought, wondering if she should say anything.

But her gran patted Laddie and said, "And now, Polly love, go and fetch Laddie the treat he's waiting for."

Polly nodded. When she fetched Laddie's chicken out she'd say she was worried she'd get burnt if she stayed outside. Then she'd go back in and write to Johnny.

"I might be mainly grey now but my hair was as red as yours when I was younger and I still have to be careful about sitting in the sun," said Gran when Polly made her excuse. "Burning easily is the downside of red hair and the pale skin that goes with it."

*

An hour-and-a-half later as she put the letter to Johnny in an envelope and sealed it with a kiss, Polly realised she'd forgotten to ask where the nearest pillar box was.

She went into the living room where her gran, Edna and Jack were listening to *Life With The Lyons*, apologised for interrupting and asked her question.

Her gran smiled. "That's all right, Polly. We've already heard it once, it's a repeat from last Thursday. Now let's see, I reckon the nearest post box is the one at the other end of Blakeley Road.

"Not the part you came down, love. Turn right out of Broome Avenue keep walking 'til you see the Community Centre. The post box almost next to it. I'm not sure what time the Sunday collection is, probably around six, though, so you should catch it if you walk quickly. And we'll have tea when you get back."

Polly hurried out. She was just passing the prefab next door when she came face to face with a friendly-looking grey haired lady carrying a small basket.

"Hello, love. You must be Peg's grand-daughter, Polly. I'm Betty Jones and I was coming to Peg's to welcome you and to see how you're settling in."

"Gran's mentioned you," Polly said. "It's nice to meet you, Mrs Jones."

"Make it, Betty, love. Sounds friendlier, that does."

"Right." Polly nodded. She knew she'd have to say something to be polite but she hoped Betty wouldn't want to stand here chatting for too long.

"I'm settling in nicely, thank you. Gran cooked a special chicken dinner and we had the vegetables from your garden. They were lovely."

"Got green fingers has my Tom," Betty said. "Flowers, veggies, fruit, you name it, they all grow for him. Looks after the flower beds in Broome Park, he does, as well as our garden and his allotment."

"That must keep him busy," said Polly. Just don't go and list the flowers, veggies and fruit, she added silently.

Betty smiled and nodded. "I've picked some of his strawberries." She pointed to her basket. "Off his allotment, these are. They'll be the last ones for this year. I thought Peg might like them for tea time."

"That'll be a real treat, Betty. And I mustn't be late for tea so I'd better go now and post my letter else I will be. I'll see you when I get back if you're still at Gran's," she added.

Thankful Betty had given her a good reason to escape, but worried Betty would think of something else to say, Polly put a spurt on. She rounded the corner on to Blakeley Road so quickly she didn't see the person coming out of number twenty-two's gate until she'd banged into him.

Polly's letter and a larger envelope he'd been holding flew to the ground as they said together, "Sorry, wasn't looking where I was going."

Glancing at him as he bent to pick up the letters, Polly guessed this was Rod - the good-looking lad with muscles her gran had talked about.

"Haven't seen you around here before, you must be Peg's grand-daughter," he said, handing her letter over. "Polly, isn't it?"

"And you must be Rod who carried a piece of furniture round for my gran," Polly replied. "Sorry again for barging into you, I was hurrying to catch the post."

He smiled. "Me, too. This is urgent."

Gran was right, Polly thought. He does seem nice, doesn't act like he thinks he's God's gift, neither.

"We may as well–" Rod began.

But he was interrupted by a voice coming from the direction of the back garden. "Rod? Rod, have you seen that small saw of mine anywhere?"

"Damn," said Rod, thrusting his envelope into

Polly's hands. "I can't let Dad see this. He'd hit the roof. Do me a favour and post it for me, Polly."

Polly glanced over Rod's shoulder and saw Mr Simmonds coming along the path by the side of the prefab. He didn't look like a man who'd fly into a rage, she thought, watching as he stopped to dead-head some roses.

"Don't say anything to Peg or Edna," Rod said, speaking quickly. "I'm off work tomorrow, if I see you around, I'll explain."

Without waiting for her to reply, he turned. "Coming, Dad," he called, going in through the gate. "I think the saw is on the shelf in the shed."

Polly hurried on her way once more. Fingers crossed she wouldn't meet anyone else who stopped her because they guessed she was Peg's grand-daughter. Oh, it was nice folk were welcoming - but let them welcome her on her way back after she'd posted the letters.

Curious about why Rod had seemed so desperate for his to go off today, she glanced down at it see who it was addressed to and wondered if he'd sealed his with a kiss like she had.

Ah, she could see the Community Centre just up ahead...

She arrived just as the postman was emptying the pillar box and, sighing with relief, passed him the two letters.

Turning, she came face to face with a pretty blonde girl who looked around the same age as her.

"Hello, are you Peg Baker's grand-daughter by any chance?"

Polly nodded, wondering how many more times she was going to be asked this question. And how did folk know to ask it anyway?

"Thought you had to be, seeing as I'd not seen you round here before. I'm Gloria Turner. Mum, Dad, *ar* kid - that's my brother Bernard - and I live on Knott Lane, the turn-off just after Broome Avenue. Peg told us you were coming to stay when she came round with the National Savings on Friday evening."

Gloria smiled. "Likely she told everyone. I don't know if it's the same where you come from but here in the prefab village everyone talks about it when someone new is moving in. I know that and we've only lived here just over a year."

"Where did you move from?" Polly asked. She'd noticed Gloria's accent was a bit different from her own or from Gran's.

"Liverpool. I'm a Scouser, I am."

"Oh, right. Well, I've not moved here for keeps," Polly said. "I will be staying about three months, though."

"Don't look so down about it. True, there's not that many around our age in the village, one less right now with my friend Rita who lives next door to your gran working away. And we are a bit cut off here. But as long as you don't mind a walk to the bus stop or train station you can get to other places dead easy. You could come dancing with me and Stan, my maybe fella, one Saturday."

"Maybe fella?"

Gloria sighed. "We're sorta not sure how we feel about each other yet. There's this other fella I like a lot and if he ever asks me out I'd I think I'd say yes in a flash. So it's a no strings attached relationship with me and Stan. But I'll get him to bring one of his friends along for you."

"I'm going steady with someone back home, Gloria. Johnny's the only one for me. He feels the same way, too. He's got his own band, "Johnny Jake and the Skifflers"."

"Never heard of them. I've heard a bit of skiffle, though. It's *orl* right. Stan puts skiffle records on at times. He's got a record stall on Radlington Market. I help out on a dress stall there."

"Johnny and his Skifflers have just won a big skiffle contest and they'll be playing at the Hippodrome for a week. You might get to hear of them after that."

"We could go to the Hippodrome when they're on, Polly." Gloria glanced at her watch. "Jeepers. Look at the time, I'm meant to be meeting a friend. Five minutes ago," she added, shaking her head.

"And I'll be late for tea," said Polly.

"Peg said you'd be starting your new job on Wednesday. I'm not at the market tomorrow or Tuesday so I'll try and call in at Peg's and we can talk some more."

"That'd be good," Polly said.

"Right, then. Ta-ra for now."

Polly smiled as Gloria hurried off and then she started to make her own, slower way back along Blakeley Road.

Gloria seemed nice. Maybe they'd get to be friends. It'd be good to have someone to confide in who, if it came to it, might cover for her if she had to keep meeting Johnny a secret from Gran. As for doing things in secret…

Polly's thoughts turned to Rod and the Miss Daphne Ormerod-Willoughby he'd written to - at a posh sounding address in London.

Could it be that Rod's Daphne was in the same boat as her having a loved one her parents didn't approve of? Polly wondered stopping to stroke a ginger cat that meowed at her from the gatepost it was sitting on.

Maybe Daphne had been packed up and sent off so she couldn't see Rod. And Rod's parents - or at least his dad - mustn't want Rod to be keeping in touch with Daphne. Or perhaps his parents didn't even know about her.

Polly glanced into the Simmonds' garden as she passed, but there was no sign of anyone. She hoped she would see Rod tomorrow. She was looking forward to hearing his story. Perhaps she'd tell him about Johnny; they'd be able to sympathise with each other.

Turning into Broome Avenue - and seeing her gran at the gate talking to Betty, Polly recalled what Gran had said about Rod not seeming to have a girlfriend and wondered what she'd say if she knew Rod's little secret.

Chapter Eight

Little White Lies
(Dick Haymes)

"'Morning, love. Glad to see you weren't called out in the night," said Peggy when Edna joined her in the kitchen. "I didn't pop my head round your door to check like I usually do in case I disturbed Polly. Mind, I was worried the noise of the washer would wake her."

"But Monday's washing day and even if it were the queen stopping here, you'd still have been up at the crack of dawn to get it done," Edna said, smiling.

It wasn't yet seven o'clock. Peggy always liked to be up early to get things going. That way, if Edna hadn't had a night call, they had time for a bit of a chat over breakfast before setting off for work.

Edna pulled down the ironing board to use as a table. "Polly's flat out. Didn't stir a muscle while I was getting ready. So it'll just be you and me for cereal and toast," she added, reaching in the cupboard for the cereal before picking up the bowls and plates from the work surface.

"That's good," said Peggy. "I told her to have a lie-in if she wanted and said to help herself to whatever she fancies for breakfast and her mid-day meal. She knows I won't be home 'til around three."

"She'll likely be glad to have time on her own to think how it'll be for her living here. She needs to get a feel for that. I expect she'll go over yesterday in her mind." Edna peered into the cereal packet. "It was a lot for her to take in," she continued, tipping *Shreddies* into the bowls.

"Meeting Jack who'll also be her boss, you explaining who lives where and then seeing a bit of the village when she went to post her letter. To say nothing of getting to know the two of us better. She didn't have much chance of that what with Jack being here most of the time but, you know Mum, when she was talking to me last night, I felt she really wanted to do that."

Peggy busied herself cutting bread for toast and putting it under the grill. It was strange how she felt a bit left out of things. Maybe that was because she was used to having Edna to herself - apart from when Jack was here of course. Then she liked to hear the two of them chatting together even if she was in the kitchen and they were in the living room. In fact, she often stayed in the kitchen to give them time alone.

It had felt different when it was Polly and Edna. That could be because it seems like Edna's getting to know Polly better and I'm not, Peggy mused as she turned the bread to toast the other side.

"You're right, Edna, it was a busy day for Polly yesterday and the pair of you stayed awake having a good old gossip for a long time after you went to bed."

Peggy bit back a sigh. She'd love to know what they'd talked about, but she wasn't going to ask. "Have a look and see if there's a jar of blackberry and apple left will you, love," she said instead. "We had a good picking last back-end and I made plenty so there should be. I feel like jam on my toast this morning, especially as we've got real butter to go on it as well."

They didn't often have butter - since it had come off ration a couple of years ago the price of it had risen steadily and it was now around twice the price of margarine. But Peggy had splashed out on half-a-pound to make Polly's first days here a bit special.

*

From the generous amount of butter being spread on the toast, Edna could tell her mother's thoughts weren't really on butter or blackberry jam. More likely she's curious as to what Polly and I were saying, she guessed. Or, more like what Polly said.

"Polly and I were talking about my wedding, Mum." Edna smiled as she poured milk onto her cereal. "Bridesmaids and dresses and flowers and that."

"From the length of time you were talking, you must've gone through the whole wedding service."

They had. And that's when Polly woke up one of my buried niggles, recalled Edna munching slowly on her cereal.

"Or did you chat about other things as well?"

Edna felt she had to share something; one thing might not go down too well, but she daren't mention the other one at all. That would really cause distress.

"She asked if Jack and I might like her Johnny and his skiffle group to play a few songs at the reception," she said at last.

"So that explains the look you had on your face. I could tell you were shilly-shallying over something."

Edna nodded and immediately felt guilty for seeming to agree. It hadn't been that she was wondering about at all.

It was the other question Polly asked after I'd told her my godfather would be giving me away, she added silently.

Polly had said, "It's sad how your dad died in the First World War so Mum you never knew him. Well, I suppose Mum knew him a bit but it happened before you were born, didn't it?"

Polly hadn't waited for a reply. She'd carried on, "It's sad for me, too, Edna. He would've been my grandad, I never even had one grandad what with Dad's parents dying years before he married Mum. He goes to put flowers on their grave sometimes. When I asked Mum about her dad's grave, she told me she didn't want to talk about it. Do *you* know where it is?"

Edna didn't. She didn't know much about her father at all. She'd been told she was conceived when he'd come home on leave – and then he'd gone back to France and, sadly, had never known about his second daughter. Her mother had always said as well that he was a lovely, kind man, the salt of the earth. That was the extent of her knowledge really.

Oh, over the years, she'd asked where he was buried, but she'd always got the same comment as Polly. She reckoned, though, he must be in an unmarked grave somewhere in France and even after all this time, thirty-seven years for heaven's sake, that's why it was too upsetting to talk about.

Which is what she'd told Polly.

And, Edna thought now, it kept me awake half the night pondering about what I'd told her and if…

"What did you tell her, Edna?"

For one awful second, Edna wondered if she'd spoken her thoughts aloud. But then her mum asked another question.

"Surely you can't be thinking of having that Johnny and his skiffle group playing at your wedding?"

"I said I'd have a think about it and talk it over with Jack. But it'd probably be best to hear them first before we decide."

"Polly and him being so far away from each other will have likely put an end to things by then anyway. She's sure to be making new friends round here and at work, too. Happen there'll be a lad she gets to like and starts going round with. Someone a bit more acceptable."

And it's more than clear that's what you're hoping for, Edna thought, glancing at her mother. Fair enough, she said she'd no intention of trying to stop Polly seeing Johnny but it's strange how she seems to be siding with Ivy over wanting it to come to an end.

That was another niggle which kept rising to the surface: the cool, almost forced, relationship between Ivy and their mum. It hadn't always been like that. She could remember while growing up in the small terraced house in Salford, where they'd gone to live when she'd been a babe in arms, how well Ivy and their mum had got on. All three of them had really.

Then one day, soon after her twenty-first birthday Ivy, saying it was so she could be nearer her job, had packed her things and gone. Edna couldn't remember any row or argument taking place so, at the time it had seemed quite a believable story. But she'd only been fifteen then.

In later years, whenever that episode rose to the front of her mind, Edna felt sure the reason Ivy had given hadn't been the whole truth. There must have been something else, something between Ivy and their mother she hadn't known about. And still didn't.

Glancing at her mum again, Edna wondered if she thought that if Polly being here put a stop to her seeing Johnny, Ivy would be that grateful it would wipe out and put right whatever had happened in the past.

She knew she was right when her thoughts were interrupted. "See, Edna, you know Ivy thinks Polly's too young to be in love. But I reckon she'd be more than pleased if Polly met someone a bit more respectable than Johnny who she liked going round with."

"Just because Johnny plays in a skiffle group it doesn't mean he isn't respectable," said Edna. "And, anyway, Polly getting to like someone new she meets wouldn't mean he'd take Johnny's place in her affections."

Polly had mentioned catching a quick glimpse of Rod and Mr Simmonds as she'd walked past their prefab and had seemed interested in Rod or, no, curious about him. But she'd also made her feelings for Johnny clear and, if Johnny felt the same way, Edna felt it more than likely that her niece would still be seeing him come the day of the wedding.

He sounded a real caring sort of lad and Edna couldn't help but think her sister Ivy was acting out of a sort of snobbishness not wanting Polly to keep seeing him. Best not mention that though.

Good grief. It was hard working out what to say and what not to say about the situation. She wasn't used to hiding her thoughts from her mother.

The sound of cheerful whistling and the chinking of bottles gave Edna the chance to change the subject. "Here's the milkman. Fancy it being that time already. I'll have to be off in a few minutes. But I'll have a slice of toast first. That blackberry jam looks delicious."

*

Polly hadn't really been asleep when her aunt got up but, feeling disorientated and all at sixes and sevens, she'd pretended to be. Although yesterday had been nice enough, she'd needed time alone to come to terms with being here for three months.

So with the murmur of voices - and the aroma of toast - coming from the kitchen, she'd lain in bed thinking and whispering to her teddy bear.

"Hopefully, there'll be a letter from Johnny tomorrow, Wilbert. And on Wednesday, I'll be starting my new job. By the following week, Johnny might have got the van and I'll be able to see him. And..."

Polly closed her eyes and daydreamed of how it would be when she and Johnny were together again.

She'd have had her first week's wages by then. Perhaps she'd buy a new dress. Another yellow one. Johnny liked her in yellow. Maybe he'd sing her his skiffle version of *The Yellow Rose of Texas*. Or if she got a blue dress he'd sing *Bonnie Blue Gal*.

Then they'd go somewhere quiet and private. Polly imagined his lips on hers and in her head she began to sing *Kisses Sweeter than Wine.*

When she opened her eyes, everywhere was quiet. Then, looking at the bedside clock, she saw it was ten o'clock and realised she must have gone back to sleep.

Knowing she was on her own now, she got up and slid out the record player from under Edna's bed. Then, childishly, she closed her eyes, ran a finger over one of the record racks and pulled out a record.

When she opened her eyes she was amazed to see she'd unknowingly made such an appropriate choice and she listened to Eddy Arnold singing *I'll Hold You in My Heart Till I Can Hold You in My Arms* while getting ready.

After eating a couple of slices of toast and drinking two cups of tea, she washed her dishes, put them away and then went into the living room. Looking out of the window she spotted Laddie who'd obviously wandered in from next door.

When he ran towards the end of the garden barking furiously, Polly saw Rod peering over the fence that separated the two gardens. Maybe he was looking for her to explain about his letter. Even if he wasn't, it would be good to have someone near her own age to talk to. True, Gloria had said she might call round. But she might just have been saying it.

*

Not wanting Rod to know she'd gone out because she'd seen him there, Polly stroked Laddie to quieten him and then said, "I thought he was trying to see off a cat so I came to stop him. I saw a lovely ginger one yesterday when I was on my way back from posting the letters."

"I was about to call round and ask you about that. Did you manage to catch the post?" Rod asked, sounding anxious.

"Got there just as the postman was emptying the box."

"That's a relief. I didn't fancy having to apologise to her for it not arriving today when I promised it would."

Polly nodded and gave what she hoped was a questioning smile.

"I couldn't help noticing it was addressed to a Daphne somebody," she said when Rod stayed silent.

"Daphne Ormerod-Willoughby," he said. "I can't imagine what she looks like with a name like that."

"You mean you've never seen her? She isn't someone your parents don't like you knowing? I thought it might be that because my letter was to my boyfriend, Johnny. And my mother doesn't like me seeing him."

"I wish it was that," Rod said gloomily. "It would make things easier in a way. They'd more than likely accept that even if it was reluctantly."

He shrugged and, although she wasn't into lads with muscles, Polly couldn't help noticing the way Rod's rippled.

"I suppose I could say I was writing to a girlfriend when I shut myself away in my room. It's hard to keep coming up with half-truths like I need peace and quiet to study plans."

"Study plans? I think you've lost me, Rod."

"I'm a brickie, Polly, and it helps to study the plans for whatever the gang and I are working on. So, I look at them for a few minutes before I–" He sighed and shook his head.

"Before you what?" Polly prompted.

Rod glanced up the garden. "My mother's somewhere around. I wouldn't want to be interrupted while I'm telling you. How about we take Laddie a walk in the park? Mrs Pearce can't take him so that gives me a good excuse for going."

Polly nodded. "Gran said she was laid up with a broken ankle."

Rod pointed to a spade sunk into some freshly-turned soil. "I've been digging over a patch so Dad can start planting his winter vegetables. I'll go and have a wash and then I'll go to the Pearces' to get Laddie's lead."

"Right," Polly said. "I'll meet you out the front in a few minutes."

It wasn't like a date, she told herself as she went indoors to smother herself in sun cream. Rod seems nice enough and I think I'm going to like him. He *is* good-looking but, like Gran said, isn't a show-off. He doesn't do anything for me, though, and I wish it was Johnny I was going for a walk with.

She had to admit, though, as she joined Rod and Laddie, she couldn't wait to hear what Rod felt he had to be so secretive about.

*

"Dad doesn't lay down the law that much," said Rod. "But at times he can be a right bigot. And one of those times is when it comes to what he sees as suitable or unsuitable careers for me and my brother. Me being a brickie is fine and our Jeff working at Burton's is all right as long as he's only there serving blokes with suits and such."

Rod took a swig of the *Tizer* he'd bought from the park's café. "But all hell let loose when our Jeff said he wanted to train as a window-dresser. Dad reckons "it's only a sissy who'd want to do summat like that"."

Stretched out on the grass with Laddie next to her, Polly glanced up at Rod. They'd walked and thrown a ball for Laddie for around half-an-hour before Rod had suggested getting something from the café and finding a spot to sit and talk.

Now they were doing that, Rod seemed to be going all round the houses instead of getting to the point of telling her about his letter to Daphne double-barrel.

"So," she said, "was your letter about Jeff? Are you trying to get him a job as a trainee window-dresser?"

Running a finger around the top of the bottle, Rod shook his head. "It was something my old man would see as far more sissyish than that."

Polly waited for Rod to continue. When he didn't she picked up a small stone and after levering herself into a sitting position, held it between her thumb and forefinger of both hands at twirled it.

"Getting blood out of this stone might be easier than getting you to explain," she told Rod.

"OK. OK. But it isn't that easy, Polly. I don't want you to think... See, what I've done, what I want to keep doing, doesn't exactly go with being a brickie and having the build that goes with it. And I wouldn't want anyone else to know about it."

"If you ever get round to telling me, I'll keep my lips sealed," she said.

"Right." Rod took another swig of his drink and then, looking, Polly thought, rather like Johnny's little niece Margaret had when she'd confessed to crying when she'd watched *Bambi,* Rod began to explain.

Chapter Nine

A Story Untold
(The Crew-Cuts)

The cake shop had been really busy with folk buying oven bottoms, Manchester tarts and such-like - probably for one last picnic before school started again after the long summer break.

And it's a right good day for a picnic, Peggy thought as she walked homewards along Blakeley Road. This warm weather isn't so good for my poor feet though, they feel like balloons that have been blown up too much. Thanks be I only work 'til two o'clock.

Peggy was about to turn into Broome Avenue, when she heard Betty calling her.

"I've been watching out for you, Peg. Thought you might fancy popping in for a natter and some fresh, home-made lemonade. I've made it fizzy with a sprinkle of baking soda and added mint leaves as well."

"Sounds really refreshing, Betty, but I really ought to get home to see Polly."

"She isn't in, Peg. I saw her in the park when I was on my way back from taking Tom his sandwiches and a cold drink. Forgot them again he did. And he's there all day on Mondays."

"She must have decided to go for a walk. Shame, if I'd know she was going to do that I'd have asked her to take Laddie."

"Oh, they did have Laddie with them."

"They?" asked Peggy. "Heck, it must be serious between them if that skiffle-playing lad's come all this way to see her when she's only been away a couple of days."

"No. You've got it wrong. Polly was with…" Betty nodded towards her neighbour's prefab.

"With Rod? Are you sure, Betty? I'd of thought he'd be at work this time of day."

"The Simmonds might have only lived next door a couple of weeks, but I knew them when they lived at number sixteen so I do recognise Rod when I see him - even from a distance. He and your Polly were sitting all cosy on a grassy slope up near that folly what looks like a temple."

"Well, isn't there a saying about being careful what you wish for? Right, Betty, seeing how there's no need to hurry home, I'd love to come in for a big glass of that lemonade. I think I need it after hearing that."

"I thought you'd be pleased your Polly has got friendly with Rod," Betty said as she passed Peggy a drink a few minutes later.

"Daft isn't it? But I just think it's happened a bit quick. I mean, however it was they came across each other, it was the first time they'd ever met and going to the park with him straight off makes our Polly seem a bit flighty."

"They might not have gone together. Happen one of them was walking Laddie for Jenny and the other one recognised Laddie and that's how they got talking."

"Then they went and sat cosied up together. That makes it seem worse."

"I wish I'd not mentioned it," said Betty, sighing. "But I reckon you're over-reacting Peg. They might've been sitting close together but they weren't hidden away all private otherwise I wouldn't have spotted them."

"That's true. I think my new responsibility just got to me a bit. I daresay Polly will tell me all about it when she gets back. And at least I won't have to punish my poor feet any more today seeing as Laddie's had a walk."

*

"Gran," said Polly, glancing at her across the living room table after they'd finished eating their chicken salad. "If you knew someone who was doing something someone else didn't approve of and–"

"You mean like you going for a walk in the park with Rod Simmonds?"

Polly looked quite taken back and Peggy realised that she'd sounded harsh and irritable. But Polly had been home well over an hour now – in fact they'd both arrived at the same time – and, although Polly said she'd been for a walk, she hadn't said where to or who with.

"I didn't mean that at all," said Polly. "I suppose your friend Betty told you? I thought she'd seen us up near the folly. That's the trouble with hair my colour. Stands out a mile. But why should anyone disapprove?"

"Because you couldn't have known him for longer than a couple of minutes, Polly. And going somewhere with him straight off–"

"I thought you liked Rod? You said he was a nice

young man. You even talked like you wanted me to get to know him."

"Maybe I did. But you didn't take any time to get to know him, did you? I wouldn't want Rod or anyone to think you were flighty, Polly."

"Rod wouldn't have thought that. He knows I'm seeing someone. Knew it before he suggested taking Laddie for a walk in the park. Laddie was here in the garden, he'd been barking at Rod over the fence."

Seems like Betty was right when she said I'm over-reacting, Peggy mused. And now I've likely gone and put up a barrier between me and Polly.

"I'm sorry, Polly love. I reckon I was making a mountain out of a mole hill. But," she added, suddenly recalling how this conversation had started, "who is the someone who's doing something someone else wouldn't approve of?"

*

Polly sighed and almost wished she hadn't brought the subject up. But after Rod had explained things, she'd come up with a way to help him - though it meant letting her gran and Edna and Jack into his secret.

She'd told him what Gran had said about how you could share a confidence with folk here and know it would be safe.

And, eventually, Rod had said, "OK, if you can think of a way of telling them without making me sound ridiculous, give it a go."

Now, though, because of the way Gran had interrupted, Polly couldn't think how to carry on.

"It's something someone's keeping a secret because not only would certain others disapprove, they'd also be upset."

The unexpected reaction those words caused scared Polly.

Her gran had made a strange noise as though she couldn't swallow and the colour was draining from her face like she was in shock.

She must be thinking I'm talking about me and Johnny, Polly thought and quickly tried to reassure, "It isn't *me* keeping a secret, Gran. It's someone else's secret I know about. It isn't something criminal or illegal or anything like that, and they said I could talk it over with you and Auntie Edna. That's what–"

"I suppose that's what you were trying to do before I started going on at you about walking in the park with Rod?"

Polly nodded and wished Edna was here. But Gran had said earlier that Edna wouldn't be in 'til later. Gran still looked a bit white-faced and she hadn't sounded like her usual self just then, either. Still, she'd likely be OK when she heard what it was.

"Tell you what. I'll make us another cup of tea, Gran, and then I'll try and explain properly."

*

Waves of apprehension continued to sweep through Peggy as she watched Polly hurry into the kitchen. Could Ivy have said something to her? In her heart she'd always been afraid that her elder daughter wouldn't keep what she'd discovered to herself.

But would Ivy really have gone and discussed it with Polly? And then told Polly to go ahead and talk it over with me and Edna? Maybe Ivy had thought Polly should know about it before coming to stay here? But why? Peggy asked herself.

Could Ivy have reckoned that Polly knowing would ruin any chance of me and Polly building up a better relationship? That would have been taking a heck of a chance, though. It could be Polly would be sympathetic and understand. Or maybe it was Ivy's way of letting Edna know what had really happened. Or…

Polly came in pushing the tea trolley. "I've brought the teapot and some extra hot water as well then we won't have to get up if we want a second cup," she said.

Peggy nodded. She'd probably need more than one cup – need it strong and extra sweet, too.

*

"So you're back, Rod. You were gone a while, you must be ready for a cuppa."

"Thanks, Mum. A cup of tea would go down well."

"Enjoy the walk, did you, son?"

"Laddie certainly did. He'll sleep well tonight with all the running to fetch his ball."

"And what did you think of the young lass, Peg's grand-daughter? Nice, is she?"

So that's what this is all about, Rod thought, stirring sugar into his tea. Mum's wondering if there's any chance I'll take up with Polly.

He was well aware his mother wished he'd find a nice girl and settle down; he just hadn't found the right one yet. As for Polly, he liked her. Liked her a lot and, if her heart hadn't belonged to her Johnny… But it did; so all they could be was friends.

His mum was looking at him, waiting for an answer. "Yes, Polly's all right," he said. Then he realised that, if Polly's idea was to come to fruition, he should maybe sound a bit more enthusiastic.

"She seems really nice, fun to be with and not self-centred like some can be."

"That's good. Maybe you could show her round a bit, help her settle in."

"Yes. Maybe." Rod drained his cup and stood up.

"Are you going to finish digging that vegetable patch now, Rod? I saw old Sam Noble earlier and he reckons it's going to rain tomorrow."

Until they'd moved, the Nobles had been their next door but one neighbours. Now, although they were only four prefabs away from the Nobles, Rod hadn't seen the gruff, elderly man for a while.

"Feel it in his bones, can he? Well, Sam's usually right when it comes to forecasting the weather. I'll go and finish digging. There's not much more to do."

*

Rod couldn't help the odd long glance across to Peg's living room. He wondered if Polly was telling her his story and then wondered if he'd done the right thing confiding in Polly.

It was strange how that had come about. He could have let her think Daphne Ormerod-Willoughby was a "forbidden girlfriend" or something. But, no, Polly had caught him when he'd felt completely cheesed off about having to keep things from his parents.

It would have been so much easier if there'd been any chance of them accepting and approving of what he was doing. His mother probably would if she knew. In fact, she'd more than likely feel proud of it; but she'd never say so, not if it meant going against Dad. So it was best not to put her in that position.

Darn it all. Rod dug hard and deep into the soil. If only his dad weren't such a bigot. Because, now, if Polly was telling Peg his secret, and if Peg agreed to Polly's plan, he'd be putting Peg and Edna in the position of going against his dad…

*

"So what do you think, Gran? Polly asked when she'd finished explaining.

I think I've had a reprieve, Peggy replied silently. Oh, without a doubt, old ghosts would come back and haunt her sleep, but for now she had someone else's problem to think about.

"I don't know Gilbert Simmonds that well," she said. "I remember Monica once telling me she'd love a little part-time job like mine but there was no way Gilbert would agree. He feels a woman's place is in the home."

"Rod said his dad was OK really but he was a bit of a bigot over some things. He'd hit the roof if he knew Rod drew…" Polly opened a comic Rod had given her and pointed, "… pictures like this. He'd think Rod was a sissy. That's why Rod has to keep it secret."

"Yes. I *can* imagine Gilbert wouldn't take kindly to a son of his doing pictures of pixies, fairies and elves and such-like for kiddies' comics. And pigs and kittens with clothes on," she added, turning the page. "He's very talented being able to draw like this."

"So would you let him come round here sometimes to work on his pictures, Gran? See, he has deadlines to keep to. His mum and dad don't go out much of an evening so he finds it hard to think up a reason for shutting himself away in his room."

"I told you how we used to call your auntie Edna "Miss Mary" when she were little because she was so good at drawing Rupert Bear and his friends didn't I, Polly? Well, she still does a few pictures when she's telling stories to the kiddies she brings here at times. Happen she could show some to Rod and he'd know if they were any good or not.

"See, she's not sure if she'll have to give up work once she's wed. If Rod thinks she's good enough maybe she could send some of her pictures off to places that produce comics and books and earn herself a bit of cash."

"Good idea, Gran. I'm sure Rod would have a look at Edna's drawings."

"But what excuse would he use for coming round here regular, Polly? I wouldn't want him telling Gilbert and Monica he was doing something for me. Not when he wasn't. And if Rod doesn't want folk to know what he's doing, what if one of my friends or one of Edna's happened to call in while he was here?"

"It needn't be that regular, Gran. I thought maybe he could come on Friday evenings when you're doing your National Savings stamps round. None of your friends would call in then knowing you were out and Edna's probably wouldn't either. She told me Jack usually comes round to listen to *Friday Night is Music Night*."

"Even so, there's still the question of what he'd tell Monica and Gilbert."

"Rod said he wouldn't have to say where he was going, Gran. They don't ask him stuff like that any more. But–"

"Polly, the neighbours would see him coming here, it would get back to them as sure as eggs is eggs."

"That's what I was about to say, Gran. See, Rod could put the paper he uses for his pictures inside record covers and if anyone does ask he could say he was coming round to listen to records with me. We'd play some to make it true." Polly smiled. "After the wireless programme of course."

"I suppose it might be all right," said Peggy. *And our Polly would realise there's other fish in the sea as well,* she thought. It would give her a new interest…

"And I could go and post Rod's pictures off for him on a Saturday morning. Then he wouldn't be in a panic about trying to catch the last post on a Sunday because he hadn't managed to shut himself away to get his work finished earlier. That's what happened yesterday when I ended up posting it for Rod along with my letter."

"Did you know what you were posting for him?"

"No. I only knew he didn't want Mr Simmonds to see it. That's why I went to the park with Rod today so he could tell me all about it without any interruption from his mum."

"I've already said sorry for going on about that," Peggy said. "And all right, love, as long as Edna agrees, we'll help Rod out. But that's only as long as Monica or Gilbert don't start mentioning anything to me. I'll already be deceiving them behind their backs and that's bad enough even if it is for a good cause. But I won't get caught up in telling them untruths to their face."

Polly smiled. "I can't imagine you ever telling real untruths, Gran."

Peggy clenched her fists beneath the table and prayed Polly would never find out the one big untruth she had told - or, rather, the untold truth.

Chapter Ten

Just Walking in the Rain
(Johnny Bragg and the Prisonaires)

"Good grief." Polly shot up in bed. "What in heaven's name is that?"

"The heavens have opened, Polly." Edna laughed. "In other words it's pouring down and when rain falls on the prefab's flat roof it sounds–"

"Like it must sound standing under a torrential waterfall in a suit of armour," said Polly, giggling now she'd got over her fright.

Edna pulled a face. "Unless it stops within the next hour, I reckon I'll need something like a suit of armour for going round doing my home visits. Last time it rained this hard it went right through my gabardine. My dress got soaked and I ended up with navy-blue skin."

She walked over to the window and pulled back the curtains. "Looks like it's set in for the day, though. Have you got anything planned?"

"Waiting for the postman to see if Johnny's written and writing back to him. And Rod's off work again today. We were going to take Laddie a walk in the park this afternoon so I could tell him if you and Gran agreed to him coming here to work on his drawings."

"It's a downright shame he feels he has to do them in secret," said Edna. "Mind, I must admit I was a bit surprised when you told me about it last night. It's much easier to think of Rod lifting weights or playing rugby than drawing pixies and elves. But those illustrations of his in the comic you showed me are really good."

"I looked at some of those comics in the living room, last night," said Polly. "I wonder if Mr Simmonds would approve if Rod did illustrations for those cowboy comics or for boys' books."

"That's a thought, Polly. You ought to mention it to Rod." Edna walked over to the dressing table, picked up a brush and began brushing her hair.

"You do realise if folk see him coming round here a bit they'll put two and two together and make five?"

"We'll know Rod isn't coming to see me. But if people want to think that it can't do any harm. I'll tell Johnny all about it when I write today. He knows what it's like when someone wants to do something their folk don't approve of."

Edna nodded. "Things can seem a bit unfair sometimes," she said, smiling at Polly through the mirror.

"Still, I always think if they're meant to be, somehow or other it works out in the end. Like the house Jack and I set our hearts on. You'd think everything would've gone ahead without hitches what with Jack being an estate agent. But there was problem after problem until we finally heard it was ours."

"So it was meant to be," said Polly.

"Yes, and before long I'll have to get down to sorting out a few things to take over there. Perhaps you'd like to help me a time or two, Polly?"

After a final glance in the mirror, she walked over to Polly's bed.

"Thing is," she said quietly, "I think your gran might feel a bit upset when she sees me packing stuff. I know she and Betty are planning on having a Saturday out at Radlington market soon - buying new outfits for when they go to see the lights at Blackpool. So…"

"You'll make a start on it then when she isn't here to see. That's a nice idea."

"I'm almost sure you'll get Saturday afternoons off, Polly. So how about you give me a hand? It would be quicker with two of us."

"'Course I will, as long as you don't make your record player and records the first things you pack up."

Edna laughed. "They'll be here for a good few weeks yet because I'll leave them until the very last. Right now, though, I better go and have breakfast. If I don't get a move on I'll be late for work."

"I'll get up in a bit," Polly said. "I'll be a working girl again tomorrow so I'll have to get up early then."

"In that case," Edna waved a hand towards the window, "I'll pull the curtains closer together. Not that there's any sun shining into the room to stop you from snoozing. But–" Breaking off she turned from the window to look at Polly.

"The postman's here. You won't want to snooze if he's delivering the letter you're hoping for. Want me to go and see?"

"Please," Polly replied, her heart beating faster in anticipation.

Edna returned quickly, "Looks like you're in luck, Polly."

Smiling, she gave Polly the letter.

"Happy reading," she said as she left the room again.

*

Polly felt under her pillow for a handkerchief to mop the teardrops from her letter. She'd read it over and over again and (even though it made her sad as well) it was good to know Johnny was missing her as much as she missed him.

He'd written a couple of newsy bits about the Skifflers, adding it wouldn't be long before they got the van and then he'd be able to come and see her. He said he could imagine the prefab village and her in her gran's prefab because she'd described everything so well in her letter to him (which he was keeping in his shirt pocket, close to his heart).

He'd ended his letter by writing out the words of the song: *Letters Have No Arms*.

As she scrubbed at her eyes, Polly heard her aunt's voice: "I'll go and get that plastic mac we bought from "Woolies", Mum. I might not get quite as wet if I put it on over my gabardine."

The next second, Edna hurried into the bedroom.

"Polly. Whatever's wrong, love? You haven't had bad news? Johnny doesn't want to stop seeing–"

"No." Polly sniffed. "I'm not that sort of upset. It's... Do you know a song called *Letters Have No Arms*?"

"Oh, that's the one about someone missing his sweetheart and feeling lonesome for a loving touch, how kisses on paper are cold and how he wants to be with her to be told the sweet things she writes about... Ernest Tubb sings it. I've got the record."

"Johnny's written the words out in his letter. That's what's made me weepy. I know it might sound silly - him missing me so much when I've only been here a couple of days, but–"

"Not silly at all, Polly. It probably seems much longer."

"It is in a way. We didn't see each other for a whole week before we went to the market together on Saturday because the Skifflers were rehearsing for that contest I told you about."

"The one they won on Saturday night?"

"Mmm. And Johnny didn't want me to go round to his uncle's cellar and watch them practising like I usually do because he didn't want me distracting him. If I'd known Mum was packing me off here, I'd have gone and watched them every flipping evening."

Then, she added silently, I'd have had more memories of him walking me home, more kisses to remember...

Edna gave a sympathetic smile. "Never mind, Polly. I'm sure the pair of you will find a way to get together soon. Remember what I said earlier about if something's meant to be.

"And now," she added, "If it's meant to be that I can prevent getting soaked to the skin, my mac will be where I think I saw it last."

Edna walked over to open the wardrobe door and Polly watched her pull out a square of grey plastic and unfold it - straightening out wrinkles and creases as she did so.

"Voila. One mac," said Edna, putting it on over her gabardine. "How's that, Polly?"

"Rather you than me, wearing that ugly thing," Polly replied.

"I'd rather be you than me and then I wouldn't have to go out in this weather. 'Bye, Polly. See you this evening."

"'Bye, Edna, and thank you for understanding."

"I might seem ancient to you but I do know what it's like being in love," she replied before dashing out with the mac rustling around her.

*

Polly had often heard that being in love made one lose their appetite. But she, she realised as her tummy rumbled, was absolutely starving. Maybe that was because the aroma of the toast Gran and Edna had obviously made for their breakfast was still wafting around the bedroom.

She could hear Gran moving around in the kitchen and decided to get up now and maybe there'd be time for them to have a cup of tea together before Gran left for work. And she'd ask if she could make some Cheese Dreams for her breakfast.

"Of course you can, love," her gran said when Polly asked the question a few minutes later.

"There's some lard and a nice bit of cheddar in the fridge. Eeh, it's a shame I've got to leave in a few minutes, I've not had fried cheese butties for ages. Just make sure you clean the cooker when you've finished, won't you?"

"I will. Is there anything you'd like me to do while you're at work, Gran? I won't be going out in this weather."

"I did some ironing earlier and I've left everything

airing on the clothes horse in the living room. You could put stuff away, Polly. Sheets and pillow cases go in the big airing cupboard in the hallway, and you could hang up my skirts and blouses in my wardrobe and Edna's in hers."

"I'll do that," said Polly. "And I'll sort out what I'm going to wear for work tomorrow as well."

"If it's raining like this tomorrow you'll have to take one of my big brollies. And a spare pair of shoes to change into like I'm doing today. I don't know about you, Polly love, but I hate having damp feet."

Polly nodded. "I'll wear my saddle shoes or my flat pumps and take my stilettoes to change into."

"Right then. I'll be off, Polly. I'm popping in next door first to see if Jenny needs any shopping. I'll be home around three o'clock."

*

Polly took another walk down Memory Lane while getting her breakfast ready - seeing herself at Johnny's house, in the kitchen, showing Stella, his mum, how to make Cheese Dreams.

They'd gone back to Johnny's after she'd watched him and the Skifflers rehearsing in his uncle's cellar. They'd played their own skiffle version of an old Music Hall song about Gorgonzola cheese.

Johnny had been starving afterwards and she'd told him about one of her favourite cheese recipes. That's how she'd ended up at his place, cooking fried cheese sandwiches with Stella. Johnny had loved the finished product.

Sighing, Polly switched on the wireless before sitting down to eat her breakfast. She didn't know whether to laugh or cry when one of the requested records played was Perry Como singing *Look Out the Window And See How I'm Standing in the Rain*.

Oh, if only Johnny were standing outside the prefab in the rain saying he loved her. Then she'd invite him in to share this morning's Cheese Dreams.

Still, even though that couldn't happen, she managed to enjoy them.

And, she thought ten minutes later as she cleaned the cooker, there aren't too many fat splashes to wipe off. After making sure everything else in the kitchen was neat and tidy she wandered into the living room to get the clothes her gran had asked her to put away.

*

"Crikey." Polly stared down in dismay at the sheets of paper that had cascaded off the shelf in the wardrobe when she'd been hanging up her gran's skirts and blouses.

The paper didn't look new and shiny – but very slightly faded and some sheets were a bit crinkled. "I hope they weren't in any special order," she murmured.

Then, as she knelt to gather them up, she guessed they must be her mum's and Edna's childhood drawings. Gran must have been rootled them out like she'd said she would.

There were picture of fairies and princesses and Rupert Bear in his red sweater and yellow checked trousers rowing a boat with a pig and a badger sitting opposite him.

Some of the pictures were really good (they must be Edna's) and others… Polly chuckled to herself.

You needed a good imagination to tell who or what they were meant to be.

And this, Polly thought, as she picked up a sheet of notepaper, must be part of one of made up stories that Gran wrote down for them.

The hand-writing wasn't easy to read and Polly wondered why Gran hadn't used block letters. But maybe she'd found it quicker the other way.

Dear Scamp with his big brown eyes and long waggy tail, Polly read.

He'll bring so much comfort to the troops. It must have been a hard and upsetting decision to let him go and be a war dog, but you did the right thing...

It suddenly dawned on Polly that she was reading part of a letter and not a story. And she shouldn't be reading it. She couldn't resist quickly scanning to the end, though, to see who had written it:

You're always in my heart, dearest Peg my darling wife

Forever yours,

Eddie

Polly quickly bundled the sheets of paper together and then stood up to put them back on the shelf in the wardrobe. After gently closing the wardrobe door, she went over to her gran's bed and sat on the edge of it.

She was surprised to feel a warm tear trickling down her cheek. But the way Eddie – who would have been her grandad if he hadn't been killed in the First World War – had ended that letter was so beautiful, so loving; it made it a bit easier, in a way, to understand why it upset Gran to talk about him.

And Scamp, too. Polly recalled how Gran had told her that she'd said goodbye to her dog in 1917. That must have been when she sent him away to be trained as a war dog.

Although Polly had never had a dog, she could imagine how awful making that decision must have been.

"I couldn't have done it," she murmured. "I couldn't have sent a pet I loved away like that."

She wondered what Gran's friends had thought. Had they thought her hard and uncaring - or had they seen it as a brave and patriotic thing to do?

Mum, thought Polly, would have only been about three at the time - too young to be told what was going on. But did she find out when she was much older? Was that why she'd never seemed close to Gran, why the atmosphere between the two of them always seemed strained?

Whatever, at least Gran had the consolation of knowing her husband thought she'd done the right thing. He'd said so in that letter. The way Eddie had written it did make him sound a lovely, kind man - just like Gran had told Edna he was. And Edna had probably been named after him, hadn't she?

Maybe, pondered Polly, I should tell Edna about the letter. But would her aunt think–?

A loud rat-a-tat at the front door interrupted Polly's thoughts and she jumped up to go and see who was there.

Chapter Eleven

Some Day My Prince Will Come (Adrianna Caselotti)

Crumbs, thought Polly when she opened the door to see Rod, wearing a biker's cap, leather jacket and denim jeans tucked into boots, standing there. *When he dresses like this, I can understand why there's a few round here carrying a torch for him.*

"Have you come out in this awful weather to see what Gran said? You'd better come in, Rod."

"Didn't you notice the rain's eased off a bit? Mum asked me to take a casserole round for Mrs Pearce while the going was good," Rod explained as he followed her into the kitchen.

"And Mrs P. asked me to drop these off for Peg." He put a package down on the draining board. "They're galoshes. Apparently, when she went to see Mrs Pearce earlier on, Peg said how she hated getting to the cake shop with wet feet. I suppose rubber overshoes are better than nothing, but proper boots would be better still."

He's talking for talking's sake, Polly thought, hiding a smile.

"Are you trying to put off the moment when I tell you Gran's answer by gabbling on about galoshes and boots, Rod?"

"I suppose." He reached for a kitchen chair and spinning it round sat astride it and rested his hands on the top bar.

Polly sighed. Johnny liked to sit the wrong way round like that.

"It isn't only wanting to know about coming round here to work on my illustrations," Rod continued. "I want to know if she thinks I'm wet."

"I take it you don't mean wet as in wet with rain," replied Polly, not trying to hide her amusement this time.

"OK. OK." Rod laughed. "Bad choice of word. But did she? Not that anyone thinking me a namby-pamby for doing them would stop me," he added.

"Well, she didn't and nor did Edna. They think you're really talented. And Gran said that, although she will be deceiving your parents in a way, as long as they don't ask her any questions about you coming round here, it will be all right."

"That's good to hear, Polly. More than good."

Standing, Rod pushed the chair away from him, walked over to Polly and gave her a hug.

He still had his arms around her when there was a tap on the back door – followed immediately by Gloria Turner stepping in.

"Jeepers," Gloria said, glaring at Polly. "You've not wasted much time, have you? I s'pose you telling me you were going steady were all a bit of eye wipe then? An excuse because you didn't fancy coming dancing with me and Stan and one of his friends. Had you already caught sight of Rod and decided to make a play for him?"

"You've got it–" began Polly.

But Gloria didn't give her a chance to finish.

"You won't make any friends round here, Polly, not if you go round telling lies an' making excuses for not going somewhere when someone asks you.

Nor for pushing yourself forward setting your cap at Rod when there's others...when you've only just come to the village."

Amazed though she was at Gloria's verbal attack, Polly wondered if it stemmed from jealousy. Was Rod the one Gloria had been talking about when she'd said there was someone she liked a lot?

But it was clear Gloria hadn't had her say yet because, glaring again at Polly, she continued, "I just hope Peg doesn't find out what you can be like. That'd be a shame because your gran's a lovely person. Good job everyone knows that then they won't judge her by the way you act."

"Hang on, Gloria," said Rod, "I was just thanking Polly for–"

He broke off and shrugged as Gloria spun around and dashed out.

"Strewth. I've never seen Gloria lose her rag like that before. And it looks like you've made an enemy there." Rod shook his head. "I'm sorry, Polly. It was my fault. I should have tried to explain as soon as Gloria came in."

"I doubt you'd have got a word in, Rod. But, as long as you, me and Johnny know that I'm not "setting my cap at you", it doesn't matter what Gloria thinks."

Polly didn't really mean that; she'd been looking forward to maybe having Gloria as a friend. She just hoped Gloria wouldn't make it hard for her to get to know others in the village.

"I suppose I better tell Gran a bit of what's happened when she comes in," Polly said as Rod was leaving. "Just in case Gloria says anything the next time they see each other."

And, Polly added to herself, I might tell Edna about that letter I found.

But Edna called in briefly to say she'd likely not be home until the early hours of the morning as one of her mums had gone into labour and when Gran got home Betty Jones was with her.

"Betty's having a bite to eat with us, Polly, love, and then we're going to listen to *The Goon Show*."

"We listen together most weeks," said Betty. "It makes it even funnier with two of us laughing at them."

Polly knew she wouldn't say anything about Gloria's visit when Betty went. It wouldn't be right to spoil Gran's evening. Maybe she'd tell Gran tomorrow.

But of course there was no time to talk the following morning and when Polly got home that evening, all Gran wanted to hear about was how she'd gone on at work.

"It's a bit different from being in the flour mill's offices, Gran. And the bus there and back was really crowded. I expect I'll get used to it all, though."

*

For the first few days Polly was too tired to go anywhere in the village of an evening so she stayed in and wrote letters - a long one in reply to the one from her mum and dad (they seemed to have settled in all right and Dad was getting stronger every day) and shorter letters to Johnny because, really, she told him most of her news when they spoke on the telephone.

The weather had changed back to being bright

and sunny and after church on Sundays Gran and Edna made a picnic and Jack took them all for a drive. So Polly didn't catch a glimpse of Gloria.

"Gloria can't of said anything to Gran," Polly told Rod one evening when she saw him doing some gardening, "Gran would've mentioned it. I'm going to stop thinking about it."

She still thought about the letter she'd seen, though, and about Eddie, the grandad she'd never known and the dad Edna never knew. She decided she *would* mention it to Edna when they were alone together.

But another couple of weeks went by and there still hadn't been a chance of telling Edna. The only time they were alone together was at night in their bedroom and Polly wouldn't have felt right talking of something like that with Gran in the next room.

They talked about Polly's job quite a lot. Edna obviously loved hearing the parts her Jack had been involved in. Talking about it made Polly feel as if she was settling down there.

*

By the end of her third full week at Ashton's Estate Agency, Polly realised she was enjoying her work.

True, there was plenty of filing and that could be boring but typing up details of properties and working out advertisements to go in newspapers was interesting.

If everybody else was busy, she dealt with telephone calls and it felt good when she could match the caller to a house that may be what they were looking for and make an appointment for them to view – or to arrange a time for Jack to go and see a property the owner wanted to sell or put up for rent.

"And yesterday," Polly told Rod on Friday evening while he sat at Gran's dining table finishing off a fairy tale illustration, "Jack, who I have to remember to call Mr Ashton at work," she added, glancing over at Jack and smiling, "took me with him to see a property that was going on our books and he let me have a go at writing a description of it."

"She made a reasonable job of it, too," Jack said. "And she's good at brewing-up. Almost as good as Edna is."

Edna laughed. "All right, I can take a hint. But you can come and help me, Jack."

"He's a right good boss," Polly said quietly as Jack and Edna went into the kitchen.

"There are two other good things about working there," she continued. "The new coffee bar, Momgambo, that's opened a few doors away and the public telephone box right outside Ashton's. It wouldn't be right to have private phone calls at work so Johnny phones me there every other day at ten past five. Sometimes he sings me a bit of a song he and the Skifflers have *skifflized* as he calls it, too."

The others who worked at Ashton's teased her a bit about Johnny but she didn't mind. She got on well with them and they often all went to Momgambo and had a coffee and played records on the jukebox before going home.

"Has Edna fixed up a time and place for her and Jack to hear the band to see if they'd like them to play at their wedding reception?" Rod asked.

"Yes, they've booked the Community Centre for the reception and Gran and Edna need to go there first to decide on decorations and work out where to put the buffet table and stuff like that. So they're going on the nineteenth for a reception rehearsal and the caretaker has agreed that Johnny and the Skifflers can go and play a couple of songs on that evening so Jack will be going, too."

"And has Johnny got a van yet?"

"He has. So I'll–"

"You'll be seeing him before the nineteenth."

"I will."

Polly pointed to Rod's illustration of Snow White and some of her animal friends. "You know the song Snow White sings in the film? Well, a week on Sunday *my* prince will come. Not on a white horse but in his van. His friend at the garage sprayed it bright orange to make it stand out. I can't wait to see it. Can't wait to see Johnny, either. It'll be thirty-six days since we saw each other."

Polly sighed. "But time will go so slowly until then."

"You'll have to find plenty to do after work, Polly. Keeping busy helps time pass quicker."

"It's my Saturday off tomorrow. I might go and buy a new dress for when I see Johnny. It's a right shame Gloria fell out with me, I could've gone to the stall she works on at Radlington market."

"I didn't know you'd had a falling-out with Gloria." Edna pushed the tea trolley into the room just in time to hear Polly's words.

"It was a while back and it was Gloria who fell out with me," said Polly and she and Rod explained between them what had happened.

"That's not Gloria's usual way at all," Edna said.

"She's well-liked in the village. I expect she felt sorry for saying such things the second she'd calmed down.

"But you could go round and see Maisie Butterworth one evening, Polly. She lives on Knott Lane. It's her stall Gloria works on. Maisie's something else again when it comes to making dresses. She'll be making your bridesmaid dress so you'd be meeting her soon anyway. She sells new from old, too, known as Maisie's "switch and twitch" dresses."

"Oh, I'll do that," said Polly.

"And I'll keep you busy tomorrow afternoon." Her aunt smiled. "Your gran will be off out with Betty. So you can help me pack a few of my things to take to my soon-to-be home."

At last, thought Polly, *I'll be able to tell Edna about that letter I saw. I hope…*

Jack's plaintive tones stemmed her thoughts. "Now Polly's time off and her wardrobe sorted, how about this cup of tea." He pointed to the big fat brown teapot. "If we don't get it poured it will be thicker than black treacle."

Polly smiled. Life was quite good right now - and would get even better a week on Sunday.

Chapter Twelve

Oh Happy Day (the Sun is Shining)
(Johnston Brothers)

Polly felt a zing of excitement flowing through her veins the second she woke. The day she'd been waiting for was here at last. Edna's bed was empty; she must have been called out to one of her mums-to-be.

It's still too early for me to get up, though, Polly thought. Maybe she should try and go back to sleep and dream about the hours ahead. But then she might over-sleep and not be ready when Johnny arrived.

She didn't feel like reading. What could she do to pass away an hour? Because then she'd have a nice long bath before breakfast and after breakfast she'd take her time getting ready so she'd look her very, very best when Johnny got here.

"It's like Christmas morning when Sarah and I were little and we knew it was too early to open our stockings, Wilbert," Polly told her old teddy. "We used to go back over things that had happened in the week and when we reached Christmas day it would be time to open them. So, I'll do a countdown from last Saturday and then it'll be time to get up..."

Polly had taken Rod's advice and done things to keep herself busy. On the Saturday morning she'd taken Laddie for a walk in Broome Park. She'd gone all the way to the main gates to see how long it took; it was where she'd planned to meet Johnny next week. In the afternoon she'd helped Edna pack some things and had told her about the letter.

Edna had cried a little. "I know it's hard to believe but your gran never told me his name, Polly. On the very rare occasions she mentioned him to me or anyone else she always referred to him as my dad or her husband.

"Sometimes I wondered if they really were one and the same. I thought maybe Mum had been seeing someone else while her husband was away fighting. But you telling me his name, well he must have been my dad. And I never knew she'd had a dog. It must have hurt her so much when she let him go to be a war dog, Scamp would have been a link to my dad for her."

Polly remembered how she'd put her arms around her aunt and suggested that Gran had let Scamp go to war because she'd felt doing that might somehow keep Eddie safe.

It didn't though, did it, Polly mused now. *And I reckon Gran has never got over losing him – or stopped loving him. Jack and Edna will have a love that lasts forever and so will Johnny and me. Oh, I hope Johnny likes my dress.*

Well, it wasn't actually a dress she was going to wear. Resting back on the pillow, Polly looked across to the wardrobe where, last night, she'd hung the brightly-patterned, orange and yellow dirndl skirt and a white shirt blouse with three quarter sleeves. She was going to knot a scarf (made of the same material as the skirt) cowboy fashion at her neck.

Maisie Butterworth had made everything for her.

"That was the other thing that kept me busy,

Wilbert, going round to Maisie's in the evenings to be measured and have fittings."

And, Polly thought, I'll be going back round there next week to decide what style bridesmaid dress Maisie's making me. She enjoyed chatting to Maisie and Maisie's husband, Andy.

Their three daughters, Dilly, who was twelve and the ten-year-old twins, had told her about their favourite wireless programmes and songs. The twins loved to hear Max Bygraves singing *Gilly Gilly Ossenfeffer Katzenellen Bogen by the Sea*.

"Gloria who lives next door and helps Mum on her market stall told them to write to Uncle Mac at *Children's Favourites* asking him to play it on the programme, Polly," Dilly had told her.

"Gloria was walking down their path when you came in at our gate. You should have said hello to her, Polly. She's right nice."

Polly had murmured something in reply. She'd thought of saying hello but then decided not to when Gloria shot her an unfriendly look.

That had worried Polly for a few minutes but then she'd told herself what with Rod being a good friend and the friends she'd made at Ashton's and talking regularly to Johnny on the telephone in the telephone box outside Ashton's, reading his letters and writing back to him, Gloria not wanting anything to do with her didn't really matter.

"Though maybe she's starting to change her mind about that, Wilbert, because Gran told me when she went round to the Turners' on Friday with the savings stamps, Gloria asked how I was settling down. And Gran said she told her I'd feel more settled after seeing Johnny when he comes today so perhaps Gloria believes I've no interest in Rod."

Polly's thoughts flicked back to earlier in the week and how, after getting back from Maisie's one evening she'd told Gran she wanted a new outfit because she wanted to look good when she saw Johnny. Gran had asked when and where she was seeing him.

Hoping Gran wouldn't say she couldn't go (because that would mean disobeying her) Polly had told her. But Gran hadn't said that – instead she'd told Polly to ask Johnny to come and pick her up here.

"Said she'd like to meet him before he and the Skifflers come to the wedding reception rehearsal, Wilbert. That was a surprise if ever there was one. But maybe Edna had something to do with it. She did tell me she was sure Gran wouldn't say I wasn't to see him even though that's what Mum seems to have hoped."

Polly felt certain her mum had been hinting at that when she'd written in her last letter: *I hope you're feeling settled now, Polly, and remember, love, your gran is acting in my place and knows what I'd want or not want for you…*

Recalling those words, a horrible thought struck Polly.

What if after meeting Johnny today, Gran decides she doesn't like or approve of him and tells me to stop seeing him? I wouldn't, of course, but it would be really good if Johnny's as welcome here as Jack is.

*

Three hours later, a surge of happiness flowed through Polly as she watched Gran chatting away to Johnny as if she'd known him for ages.

Edna, who'd got home a short while before Johnny arrived, smiled across at Polly and sent her a quick thumbs up.

Polly was even more delighted when her gran told Johnny to make sure he came in when he brought Polly back from wherever they were going.

"We're going to the park," Polly said. "There's loads of it I haven't seen yet. Dilly Butterworth told me there are squirrels in the woods and sometimes they'll take a nut from your fingers."

She smiled. "That's why I bought some hazel nuts yesterday."

Johnny smiled back at her. "I'm taking you somewhere else first, Polly."

Then turning to her gran again said, "I'll be bringing Polly back around seven o'clock. It's a bit of a drive home and I've got to get home to rehearse a couple of songs the Skifflers will be performing tomorrow night."

"Have you got a new booking?" Polly asked.

Johnny nodded. "We have. I'll tell you about that later."

"If you get here a bit before seven I'll have a bite of supper ready," Gran said.

"Do you like fruit cake, Johnny? I made one yesterday."

"I'll make sure I'll have time for a slice of that," he replied, smiling.

"That'll be good," Polly said. "Rod told us on Friday the comic place he does pictures for have asked him to do an extra one. If his Mum and Dad aren't going out, he's coming round to make a start on it so you might get to meet him, Johnny. But now—"

"Now, if you stand here chatting much longer, you'll still be here at seven," Edna said.

Polly threw her a grateful glance. Edna had obviously sensed how impatient she was feeling.

"Off you go then, Polly love," her gran said. "We'll see you both later."

As she and Johnny walked down the path Polly slipped her hand through Johnny's arm and squeezed it tight. "I think Gran like you," she said.

Johnny grinned and sang a silly version of an Eileen Barton song. "*She knew I was coming, she baked fruity cake, fruity cake.*"

He opened the van door for her and after she'd got in, he bent down and gave her a quick kiss on the cheek. "I've missed you so much, Pippi," he said.

"Me, too," Polly replied.

She didn't dare pull him closer and kiss him the way she wanted to in case Gran, or any of the neighbours, were watching from their windows. But she'd do that when they were properly alone. Her toes curled inside her shoes and her heart beat faster as she watched him walk round the van to the driver's side.

*

"Well, Mum, I'll be blowed if I know why Ivy's so against Polly's young man," Edna said after they'd watched the van drive away.

"I don't, either. He's a pleasure to talk to and he's

respectful as well. Fair enough his hair is a far cry from short back and sides and those jeans, clean though they were, aren't exactly smart. But I suppose it's all the rage to dress that way."

"Lads his age want to emulate James Dean. It'll be even more popular now what with him getting himself killed last week in that awful car crash. Barbers and jeans manufacturers will be quick to cash in on that tragedy," said Edna.

"As for Johnny, he obviously thinks the world of our Polly. You can tell by the way he looks at her. And as well as phoning her every other day, he writes regularly, too." Edna moved away from the window to put the kettle on for a cup of tea.

"I wonder if Polly will keep his letters," she continued. "I've got every single one Jack sent me when he was away on that course and you know, Mum, I've still got the ones Robert wrote as well. Even though the war took him, there'll always be a small piece of him in my heart. Love letters mean so much, don't they?"

Edna felt sure her mother must have kept more than the one letter Polly had found and hoped her mother might talk about them now. It would be so good to hear something about the father she'd never known.

However, there was no response to her question and, mentally shrugging, Edna poured the boiling water into the teapot and reached into the cupboard for cups and saucers.

*

As Peggy stirred her tea, she thought of the wonderful letters her Eddie had written during the

First World War. She'd kept them in a large old chocolate box behind the old leather satchel on her wardrobe shelf.

She'd opened the chocolate box and taken some out a couple of weeks back after she'd pulled the satchel down to find the pictures Edna and Ivy had drawn when they were little.

It was years since she'd read any of Eddie's letters but the raw and bitter grief when reading of his love for her – his loneliness without her and the yearning in his heart – had still been as strong as ever.

And now, she thought crossly, *Edna's gone and brought that feeling right back.*

Mind, Edna probably had similar feelings when she thought of Robert, or read the letters she said she'd kept. Thankfully, though, Edna had found love again, but wars had brought so much heartache to folk.

Love could bring heartache, too. Especially if someone tried to stand in the way of love like Ivy had tried to do with Polly and Johnny. It would likely drive an even bigger rift between herself and Ivy when Ivy found out Johnny was still very much on the scene.

It was because of the way the lad had been keeping in touch with Polly that had made her suggest him coming here to fetch Polly today, Peggy mused. True, she'd have been meeting him when he and his skiffle band came to the Community Centre so Edna and Jack could hear and see them perform before deciding if they'd play at the wedding reception, but she'd wanted to meet Johnny before that.

And although she'd never hadn't had any intention of forbidding Polly to see him like Ivy had seemed to hope, she hadn't at first been thinking of making it easier for them to meet.

She wouldn't have done, either, if she hadn't liked what she'd seen today. But, as Edna had said, it was obvious Johnny thought the world of Polly. So when they came back from their outing she'd tell Johnny he was welcome to come round to see Polly whenever he liked.

Fingers crossed she was doing right and, even though Polly and Johnny were young, that this was the real thing for both of them. Because…

Sometimes first love could be the only love. She just hoped nothing would happen that'd mean Polly ending up with a broken heart the way she had.

Chapter Thirteen

Two Hearts, Two Kisses, Make One Love
(Pat Boone)

"So where are you taking me, Johnny?" Polly asked. She was sitting as close as she could to him with her hand on his leg and Johnny covered her hand with his whenever he wasn't changing gear.

Johnny laughed before singing a few lines of an old Music Hall Song about the okay thing on Sunday was walking in the zoo.

"You're taking me to a zoo?" Polly was surprised and a bit disappointed. That didn't sound very romantic. Besides, she wasn't keen on zoos.

"It's an amusements park as well with fairground rides and other things. Graham took his girlfriend last week and he said the ghost train ride lasts for ages. We'll be able to snuggle up close together in the dark, Pippi."

"That sounds more like," she murmured.

He squeezed her hand and turned his head for a quick smile.

Oh, how she loved the curve of his lips and the way his eyes crinkled at the corner when he smiled.

"There are two other reasons I'm taking you there, though. I want to show you the big hall where they have concerts and other music events. It's where the Skifflers are performing tomorrow night. It'll only be during the interval but–"

"Lots of people will hear you and you might get

some more bookings," said Polly. "Are you going to do a skiffle version of that walking in the zoo song?"

"I'll sing you one of the numbers we'll be doing when we get there. Not in the hall itself but somewhere else. You'll have to wait and see. But it's the other reason we're going. We'll go on the ghost train first, though," he added, squeezing her hand again.

"I hope we get there soon," Polly said. She couldn't wait to feel his arms around her and have his lips on hers.

*

There was a tingling in the pit of Polly's stomach as she sat close to Johnny on the hard wooden seat in one of the ghost train's carriages. Any second now they'd be going into the tunnel where it would be dark and nobody would be able to see them.

It seemed ages before the carriage zoomed forward but once they were inside the tunnel, Johnny put his mouth close to her ear. First he told her how much he missed her when they were apart, how he read her letters to him over and over and how talking on the telephone was bitter-sweet because he couldn't see her or hold her.

Before she could tell him she felt exactly the same way, his lips moved across her cheekbone in a series of kisses as tender and light as a summer breeze. He kissed the tip of her nose and then his mouth moved up to her eyes and he kissed each one before tracing a path downwards.

His kisses were so sweet and tender they sang through her veins. And, finally, the lingering longer kisses her eager lips were waiting for.

Polly gave him back kiss for kiss, savouring every moment. She wanted the ride on the ghost train (where there must be ghosts, spiders and other scary things because she was vaguely aware of folk in other carriages screaming) to last for ever.

But, all too soon, the carriage left the dark tunnel and they were out in the open again.

When they climbed out of the carriage her knees were trembling so much she had to cling on to Johnny's arm. She could feel his uneven breathing war against her cheek as he pulled her closer against his side.

They both laughed when someone waiting to get on the ride said, "Gosh, it must be scary, she can hardly stand up."

*

After he'd taken her to see the King's Hall where the Skifflers would be performing, Johnny, his arm around her shoulders, led Polly to what he told her was his other reason for bringing her here.

"It looks a bit like a telephone box," she said. "And there are slots and buttons and things. But…"

Johnny smiled. "You're right, it looks like a telephone box outside and on the inside. We'll go in, pick up something that looks rather like a telephone and put money in a slot. It won't be a phone call to someone we're paying for, though. Come on, Pippi, and I'll show you."

They stepped inside; there wasn't much room but Polly didn't mind that at all.

"You wanted to hear what the Skifflers will be doing tomorrow," Johnny said, picking up the piece that looked like a telephone. "This is a microphone and after I've put my money in the slot, a light will come on just there." He pointed.

"Don't talk when it comes on Polly, but you can join in with the song if you like."

"Which song?" she asked, puzzled.

"You'll see and hear in a minute. But don't say anything else now," he told her, putting a coin in the slot.

Polly stared at the place he'd pointed to and a couple of seconds later saw a green light.

Then Johnny began to sing. It was a Pat Boone song called: *Two Hearts, Two Kisses, Make One Love*. It was about love setting the world afire and sparks burning inside and one kiss feeling nice but two kisses were paradise.

Polly wasn't sure why Johnny was standing inside this kiosk singing to her, but she loved the look in his eyes as he sang the words and joined in with the chorus – which were the same words as those in the title.

"That's it. Done," Johnny said, after a small beeping noise. "And…"

Polly gasped as something appeared out of the machine.

"It's a record," Johnny said, laughing as he handed it to her. "I think it's only big amusement parks like this that have these booths where you can cut a record. You'll be able to play it on that portable player you told me your aunt Edna's got.

"And while you're listening to it you'll think of our two hearts beating with love for each other," he added.

"Oh, Johnny." Polly sighed as Johnny licked away the errant teardrop rolling down her cheek.

"I'll play it over and over," she said as they stepped out of the kiosk. "It will make me feel closer to you on all the days we're apart."

"That won't be as many days this time, Polly. We'll be seeing each other at the Community Centre on the nineteenth. That's only ten days off."

"I know and that'll be nice but it won't be just you and me together alone."

"There's still two or three hours left to spend together alone today, Polly. I told you before how Broome Park is my lucky park so we'll go back to the van and drive there now and see if I'll be lucky enough to get a few more kisses from my best–"

Before Johnny could finish speaking a little girl, who looked to be around seven, ran up to them and tugged Polly's arm.

"I've gone and got lost," she said. "And I'm not to speak to people I don't know but I saw you one time before, I know I did. Will you help me find Mummy and Daddy?" she added, tears rolling down her cheeks.

"Of course we will," said Polly. "Where did you see them last?"

"My sister was waiting for a ride on Lil the elephant. I don't like elephants they're too big so I thought I'd go and see the monkeys. I didn't tell Mummy or Daddy and now–" She started sobbing in earnest.

Johnny crouched down in front of her. "My name's Johnny," he said. "And you think you've seen Polly before. I'm Polly's friend so will you tell me your name?"

"It's Anne Ogden."

"Well, listen, Anne. There's a place here for lost children to go and I expect your mummy and daddy will be waiting for you there."

"Don't want to go to a place for lost children," Anne wailed.

Polly wasn't sure what to do or say next.

She needn't have felt worried though because Johnny, in his lovely, gentle way, calmed the little girl with the words, "All right, sweetie-pie, you don't have to. How about you just stay with Polly and I'll go and see if I can find them and bring them back here?"

Anne sniffed and nodded.

"Have your mummy and daddy got a gramophone - a machine thing for playing records on?" Johnny asked her.

"There's one at the house we're stopping in," said Anne.

Johnny rose and putting some coins in Polly's hand said, "Take her into the magic telephone box and sing some nursery rhymes, while I find her parents, Polly," he said, and then hurried off.

Anne was still a bit tearful when Polly guided her into the kiosk. But she cheered up a little when Polly explained that after they'd sung some songs a record would come through a slit and Anne would be able to take it home with her and play it on the gramophone.

"But," said Polly, aware that it wouldn't take that long to cut a disc, and Johnny might take a while to find Anne's parents (he'd have to get a call put out over the loud speakers if they weren't at the lost children's office), "I think we'll have a little rehearsal first before we sing into the microphone bit."

So they sang a few nursery rhymes and then *Ten Green Bottles*, because that was a long song, before Polly put a coin into the slot.

Anne was thrilled when the record slid out and when Polly turned towards the door, she smiled as she saw Johnny hurrying up with a frantic-looking woman.

She gently pushed Anne in front of her and waited a couple of seconds while the little girl was hugged tightly by her mother.

And Polly was amazed as she joined them and recognised the woman when she looked up. It was Janice, her mother's friend. The one who was renting the house. And Janice recognised her, too.

"You might see Mrs Baines and some of your other neighbours from Curzon Street, Polly. We're on a charabanc outing," said Janice. "But it's amazing that it should be you Anne asked to help her. She couldn't have known it's your house we're living in at the moment."

"Anne did say she'd seen me before," said Polly. "Maybe it was when I came and met Mum from work one day and we went into a café and you were there. You did have a little girl with you, it must have been Anne. It was quite a bit ago, she'll have grown since then, that's why *I* didn't recognise *her*. And I don't think I ever knew your surname so no bells rang when Anne said she was called Anne Ogden."

"Well, I can't thank you and… and…" She waved a hand towards Johnny. "Sorry, I was in such a panic I never asked your name."

"He's called Johnny," said Anne who had obviously recovered completely now she was safe with her mum. "I like him. He's nice."

"I can't thank you and Johnny enough for looking after Anne," Janice continued. "Won't you both come back to the lost children's office where my husband and Anne's sisters are waiting for me? The girls were in a bit of a state, Polly," she added, "I thought it would be quicker for me to come on my own. But I'm sure they and my husband will want to thank the two of you for taking care of Anne."

"No, really, Mrs Ogden, it's nice of you to ask but we've really got to get back. Polly's gran is making us a meal," said Johnny.

"But," Johnny said to Polly after Janice went off after telling them both to come and see her if Polly was visiting near her home, "before we go to your gran's, Pippi, there'll still be time to spend an hour or so in Broome Park."

"Where you might be lucky enough to get some kisses," said Polly, smiling up at him before they set off once more to Johnny's van.

*

Although towns were more her thing, Polly thought she could easily become a country loving girl if it meant meandering through glorious woodland with Johnny's arm around her.

They'd passed a park gardener tending a bonfire before reaching the woods and now the smell of wood smoke mingled with the scents of autumn earth. The leaves on the trees and underfoot were deep bronze, gold, copper and scarlet: "Like some of the colours in your skirt, Polly," Johnny said, before pointing to a fallen tree trunk and suggesting they sat for a while.

"I'll throw a couple of nuts down and keep one between my finger and thumb," said Polly. "Then if the squirrels come I'll see if I can get one to eat from my fingers."

"I've a much better idea." Johnny lifted her hand towards his mouth. "*I'll* eat from your fingers." And, after sucking a tiny nut into his mouth, he nibbled each one of her fingertips.

Any thoughts of squirrels forgotten, Polly turned into his arms and soon became lost in the dreamy intimacy of their kisses…

*

A while later as they were walking back towards the place where Johnny had parked the van, Polly pointed to a small, noisy crowd of people.

"They're probably watching the Broome Park tug-of-war team practising for next week's contest," she said.

"I think I told you about it the other day when we were talking on the telephone, Johnny. Rod's on the team. That's mainly to please his dad. Rod didn't really want to take part because he's starting to get the extra commissions for his drawings and needs time to do them. But, of course, he can't tell his folks that."

"Crikey, Polly. I'd go crazy if I had to keep what I do a secret from my parents. I'm lucky they, and you, understand I need time for rehearsing and performing at places."

"It's a right good job Gran lets Rod come round to work on his illustrations," Polly said. "He wouldn't be able to get them done, else. I hope they finish tug-of-war practising in time for him to come round this evening."

"She's a good sort is your gran. Seems like she judges things for herself and if she thinks someone, or what someone is doing, is all right she gives a helping hand."

"Or some of her special fruit cake," Polly said. "And we'd best be getting back to Gran's else you won't have time to eat it."

They hadn't walked much further when Polly heard someone call her name. Turning, she saw Gloria Turner hurrying towards them.

Remembering the last time Gloria had spoken to her (and the time she hadn't but had given her an unfriendly look) Polly couldn't help but feel apprehensive. Why would Gloria want to say anything to her now? Gloria must know it was Johnny she was with because Gran had told her he was coming today.

What if Gloria says the same sort of things she said when she came round to Gran's that day and saw Rod with me? Polly thought. I mean Johnny knows about that because I told him. But, even though he must know it isn't true, it won't be very nice if Gloria tells him she thinks I'm "making a play" for Rod, "setting my cap" at him.

As Gloria came to a stop beside them, Polly took a deep breath.

She really didn't want anything to spoil this precious time spent with Johnny.

Chapter Fourteen

Wrap Your Troubles in Dreams
(Frank Sinatra)

"Polly, I just want to apologise for ignoring you the other day when you was going to Maisie Butterworth's. I'd just heard about James Dean getting killed and honest to god, I were that upset…"

Gloria paused and gazed up at Johnny before looking at Polly again. "This is your Johnny, isn't it? He puts me in mind of James Dean in the photos in the film magazines. Now I've seen him, it's easy to understand that you aren't interested in Rod Simmonds.

"Jeepers. Maybe I shouldn't of said that. Take no notice of me. Mam's always telling me I've got a mouth as big as the Mersey Tunnel. I'll go back and cheer Rod's team on now. Ta-ra for now, Polly."

Polly watched silently as the other girl walked away. She couldn't make up her mind if Gloria really had come over to apologise for the other day - or if she'd used that reason as an excuse to try and stir things by mentioning Rod like that.

What had Johnny thought of it?

Polly glanced at him and was surprised to see he was grinning.

"Talk about a dizzy blonde," he said. "Graham's girlfriend's like that. Speaks without thinking sometimes and it makes her appear spiteful. She isn't really, though."

"I don't *think* Gloria is, either," said Polly. "Edna said she's well-liked in the village. Dilly Butterworth said she was right nice, too."

"So we'll give Gloria the benefit of the doubt then. But standing here talking about her is using up time. If we don't hurry, Pippi, I won't be able to do justice to your gran's fruit cake."

Laughing, Polly agreed and they ran the rest of the way to the van.

*

It was almost eight o'clock when Johnny thanked Polly's Gran for the delicious supper and said goodbye to her and Jack and Edna.

Polly was delighted to hear Gran reply, "You're welcome, lad, and call any time you like to see our Polly."

"Maybe seeing as Gran obviously thinks you're the bees' knees, Mum will start approving of you, too," Polly told Johnny as they walked down the path.

"What's not to approve?" he asked, laughing.

"I think it's you having a skiffle band she doesn't approve of more than you yourself. If you do get to play at Jack and Edna's wedding reception, and I'm sure you will, you'll have to do some ballads and what Mum considers proper music as well."

"I'm sure we'd win your mum over with our version of *Wake the Town and Tell the People*," Johnny said, "even if the sound of the wedding bells is made by me on the old washboard."

Polly sighed. "I do miss sitting in your uncle's cellar watching and listening to the Skifflers."

"I miss walking you home afterwards, Pippi, and saying goodnight with a silvery moon peeping from the dark sky. It isn't really dark enough to give you a goodbye kiss now, is it?"

"Gran, Edna and Jack are listening to *Star Bill*, so they wouldn't see if you did. And the van's in the way of anyone from the prefabs opposite seeing."

Polly glanced towards the prefab next door and, to her dismay, saw Gloria and another girl coming out of the Pearces' with Laddie.

"Why did they have to come out right now?" she said.

Johnny shook his head before kissing a finger then running the same finger down Polly's cheek. "We'll have to make up for no proper goodnight kiss next time. And that won't be long," he added as he opened the van door and got in.

He set off, giving a light toot on the horn as he passed the Pearces' gate and Polly saw Gloria wave.

"I don't think you've met Rita yet?" said Gloria walking up to Polly and then introducing the two girls.

"I'm only home for a long weekend," Rita said. "But I'll be back for good at the end of the month. We'll have to get together then if you're still staying at Peg's."

"And you and me should go somewhere one evening, Polly," said Gloria.

Still not too sure of Gloria, Polly looked down at Laddie and stroked his head.

"Listen, Polly, honest, I never meant to cause trouble when I spoke to you on the park this afternoon. I just didn't think how it might sound until I'd said it. And I know I were right out of order that day when I came round to Peg's. I'm sorry about that an' all. Only, well, I told you there was a fella I like a lot and–"

"And it's Rod?" said Polly.

Gloria nodded. "The green-eyed monster took over when I saw you and him sorta together."

"She's had a thing for Rod ever since she first set eyes on him," said Rita.

"Yes but that's no excuse for me saying what I did to you, Polly. So…?"

"So, apologies accepted and, yes, we should go somewhere one evening, Gloria."

"Maisie said how you'll be going round on Tuesday to choose a style for the bridesmaid's dress she'll be making for you, so I'll pop in as well and we can fix something up," said Gloria.

Laddie whined and pawed at Rita.

"He's telling you he's fed up of waiting for his walk," said Polly.

Rita laughed. "All right, boy, now Gloria's made things up with Polly, we'll go. I'll see you in a few weeks, Polly."

"And I'll see you Tuesday," Gloria said as she and Rita hurried off with Laddie pulling on his lead.

So, thought Polly as she made her way indoors, I reckon this has been the best Sunday I've had since I came here. Mum might not be too pleased if she hears about Gran telling Johnny he could call in any time, though. I hope it won't cause any more tension between them if she does.

Still, she thought, as a guest on *Star Bill* started to

sing just as she went into the living room, I'll do what it says in this song and wrap that trouble up and dream it away.

*

Polly had woken late and hadn't had time to make any sandwiches to take to work. She'd been planning to take sandwiches every day this week to try and save a bit of money. She'd spent quite a lot on the outfit Maisie made her.

Today, Jack was sending her out with one of his staff. Even though Polly was only temporary he said she should see how everything was done in case she ever decided to become an estate agent herself.

"Seeing as I've not brought sandwiches, I'll have to go to the Momgambo," Polly told Irene at lunch time. "Else, when I come with you to show that couple over *Tall Trees* this afternoon, my tummy will be rumbling."

Irene's job was to show a property for sale at its best advantage and Polly was curious to see how that would be done at that at this particular house. She'd gone there with Jack last week to take down particulars. It hadn't been very well cared for so it would need a lot of time and work spent on it. It didn't have any trees in the garden - let alone tall ones.

"Don't be late back, Polly," Irene warned. "We'll need to leave at two-fifteen."

"I can only afford one coffee and a couple of biscuits," said Polly. "I won't even be playing a song on the jukebox so, as Gran would say, I'll be back quicker than a flick of an ant's eyelid."

Polly had meant what she'd said about being

quick. But the first thing she saw when she walked into the coffee bar was a notice announcing a live performance from a country and western duo: *Here at the Momgambo on Saturday 15th October.*

"Are you going to have live performances as a regular thing, Kenneth?" she asked the man behind the counter. "Because if you are, you'll have to book Johnny Jake and the Skifflers. They won a skiffle contest a while back.

"They'll be playing at the Hippodrome for a week soon, but they're already getting loads of bookings. They're really good, they don't only do skiffle they do other stuff as well. They're on at the King's Hall tonight and–"

"Hold your horses, Polly. It isn't down to me. I'm just the manager here. Wilf, who owns the place, makes decisions like that."

"Where can I find him? Will I have to write to him or does he ever come here?"

"I think you've seen him a time or two already. The jukebox belongs to the company Wilf works for. They make and import them. He comes to collect the money and change the records over and check everything's working all right."

"You mean that man who always plays The Harmonicats over and over while he's here? The…the one I spilt coffee over once. Oh, say it isn't him you mean, Kenneth. He was ever so nice about it but–"

"That's him. And talk of the devil." Kenneth winked and pointed over Polly's shoulder.

Polly swung round to see the man smiling.

"Wilf," said Kenneth. "This is Polly, she works at the estate agent's a couple of doors down. Regular customer she is. You probably remember seeing her," he added, grinning. "She wants to know if you'll book a live performance from... What did you say they're called, Polly?"

"Johnny Jake and the Skifflers," Polly said breathlessly.

"Can't say I've heard of them," said Wilf.

"They won a big skiffle contest and they're performing at the King's Hall tonight and they've lots of other bookings, too."

"I've heard Lonnie Donegan doing some of that skiffle music," said Wilf. "It might go down all right in here. I'd need to hear them first. Tonight's no good. I've already got someone to see."

"Could you come to the Broome Park Village Community Centre on the nineteenth? They're playing a few numbers then, though it won't be in front of a proper audience. It's a rehearsal for my aunt's wedding reception so there'll only be her, her fiancé, my gran and gran's friend who'll be helping with the buffet and– "

Polly, aware she was babbling, broke off.

Wilf laughed. "Never could resist a lass with red hair, even one who spills coffee over people," he said, digging into a pocket and pulled out a diary. "Nineteenth of this month?" he asked, flicking through the pages.

"About eight o'clock," said Polly, crossing her fingers.

"Right. I'm free then. Near Broome Park, is it? I know where it is. I was brought up not far away so I used to go there regularly before the war. "First World war, that was. Always meant to go back but I ended up living in the Big Smoke."

"You mean London? You'll be coming from London?"

"No. I moved back to Prestwich a year or two ago. Came to keep an eye on my old Ma. She's well into her eighties now. Still lives in the house I grew up in."

"So, you'll be able to find the Community Centre all right," said Polly. "It's right at the end of Blakeley Road."

"I'll find it." Wilf nodded.

"Oh, thank you," said Polly. "I'm sure you'll like them. And seeing them while they're performing is better than listening to a song on a jukebox. That's why it would be good for business if they perform live here.

"And Johnny Jake and the Skifflers are as good if not better than The Harmonicats you seem to like so much," she added, smiling. "I love the words in that song - especially the line "Come make your home in my heart"."

"Yes, that song is special to me," said Wilf, "and something tells me one of the skiffle lads is special to you?"

Polly felt herself blushing. "Yes, Johnny Jake is my boyfriend. But I'm not just saying they're good because of that."

Wilf laughed. "Time will tell, Polly lass. Time will tell."

"Crikey, talking of time. I'll have to dash. Sorry

Kenneth, can't stop for my coffee. I'll call in after work and make up for it then. And, I'll see you on the nineteenth," she said to Wilf, before hurrying out.

Gosh, wouldn't she have something to tell Johnny when he phoned on Wednesday.

And I'll have to tell Jack and Edna and Gran, Polly realised. She hoped they wouldn't mind Wilf coming along to the rehearsal for the wedding reception.

Chapter Fifteen

Happy Talk
(Ella Fitzgerald)

"Are you sure you don't mind, Edna?" Polly asked. "I mean, I couldn't ask you about it first. I had to grab the chance while I had it."

They were in the kitchen washing up after their meal. Gran was out. Polly had been relieved when she'd got in to hear Gran had gone to the pictures with Betty. It had meant she could tell her aunt about Wilf when the two of them were on their own. She was sure Edna would understand and make it all right with Gran and Jack.

"I know it wasn't really right asking a stranger to turn up while you're making plans for your wedding reception," Polly added, passing Edna a plate to dry. "But I did say to come about eight o'clock, so you might have worked everything out by that time. And he's a lovely man."

"Is he now?" Edna raised an eyebrow.

"Not like that," said Polly. "He's got silvery-grey hair and he must be in his sixties, I should think."

"Of course I don't mind him coming, Polly. Jack won't, either. It could be a good chance for the Skifflers if this Wilf of yours likes them."

"What about Gran, though? Will she mind? I know having everything right at your reception is important to her. She might not like a stranger being there while she's working everything out."

"She'll be listening to your Johnny anyway, so I can't see she'll mind someone else doing the same. And if this Wilf wants to talk business with Johnny and the band after he's heard them, they can always go to The Woodman's and leave the rest of us at the Community Centre."

"You know, Edna," said Polly, "I was really cheesed off when Mum told me I was to come and stay here while she and Dad are in Wales. I didn't think I'd get to see Johnny at all. But that's worked out all right. Plus if I hadn't been here and working for Jack, I'd never have known about the Momgambo. And Johnny wouldn't have had this chance of playing there. Just think, if Wilf likes them they could become the Momgambo's resident band."

Edna smiled. "What did I tell you a bit ago? Things have a way of working themselves out if they're meant to be."

"I wish it was meant to be I could tell Johnny the news face to face on Wednesday instead of on the phone. And I don't know that Mum will see anything as being meant to be when she knows what's going on," said Polly.

"I must write to her tonight if I can think of anything to say. I don't want to mention Johnny but most of my news is about him so there isn't much left to tell her."

"Tell her you're going to Maisie's tomorrow to decide on your bridesmaid dress. It's a shame Sarah decided not to be one of my bridesmaids, but I understand her feeling she couldn't keep leaving the baby to have fittings for it and it would be too far for her to bring him with her."

"But she'll come to the wedding, Edna. She told me that in her last letter. That's something else I can tell Mum. I bet our Sarah hasn't had time to write to her very often."

"See, everything's coming up smelling like roses after all," said Edna. "And that's the pots done and put away. It's nearly half-seven. Time for *Journey Into Space*. I can't get used to Alfie Bass as Lemmy, though. I just keep visualising him as he was in *The Lavender Hill Mob*.

"Anyway, how about we have another cuppa while we listen to it and then you can go and write your letter?"

They'd only just sat down when there was a knock on the front door.

"I'll go," Polly said. She really wasn't too bothered about listening to the programme.

When she opened the door she was surprised - and more than a bit apprehensive - to see Rod and Mr Simmonds standing there.

Rod's father being with him explains why they've come to the front door and not the back door, Polly thought. Mr Simmonds will think it's more proper. But, crikey, are we in for a show-down? Has he found out-?"

"Is your gran home, Polly?" Rod asked.

Polly saw that he was smiling and he wouldn't be if his dad was annoyed, would he?

"She's gone to the pictures with Betty Jones. But Edna's in if you'd like to see her?"

"I understand Miss Baker, as well as you and your grandmother, helped and encouraged Rodney in his artistic endeavours," said Mr Simmonds. "So, yes, if she is available, I would like to speak to Miss Baker and yourself, young lady. Then you could pass my gratitude onto your grandmother."

"Well, please come in then," said Polly.

*

"It was Rod's picture of cowboys, that did it, Gran," Polly said later that evening. "Mr and Mrs Simmonds had gone out but Mr Simmonds went back unexpectedly because he'd forgotten something and he caught Rod working on his illustration."

"And, apparently," Edna said, laughing, "Mr Simmonds is a huge fan of Westerns and John Wayne and must have thought it a *manly* thing to do illustrations for cowboy magazines."

"So then, after he'd heaped praise on Rod," Polly added, "Rod confessed to doing his other sort of illustrations, too, and how he'd come here to work on them because he hadn't thought his dad would approve. And he told him it was us who suggested him doing illustrations of cowboys."

"And," said Edna, "Rod explained how he'd very cleverly told Mr Simmonds that he'd got the commissions for cowboy illustrations mainly because of his contributions to the comics that have stories about animals and fairy tale characters."

"Rod told us his dad thought a bit about that," Polly said, "then Mr Simmonds said that Walt Disney hasn't done too badly out of animals and fairy tale characters and if Rod wanted to make a career out of illustrating and such-like he had his blessing."

Polly laughed when her gran came out with one of her sayings:

"Well, I go to the foot of our stairs. Leastways, I would if we had stairs," she added, joining in Polly's laughter.

"It might help Rod's brother, Jeff, to get permission to become a window-dresser, too," Polly added. "Especially as Jeff will be helping Rod... You tell her that bit, Edna."

"Rod's offered to paint a sort of wedding mural on paper to go on one of the walls in the Community Centre, Mum, and to make some decorations for the reception as well. And Jeff is going to help display them."

"It's Rod's way of thanking you and Edna for letting him come here to work on his illustrations, Gran," said Polly.

"That was down to you, Polly love," Gran said.

"There's something else that's down to our Polly as well," said Edna. "Something she's fixed up for Johnny."

And Edna went on to explain about Wilf coming to the reception rehearsal.

*

"I was worried Gran wouldn't like a complete stranger coming to the Community Centre," Polly told Johnny as she stood in the telephone box, the telephone pushed hard against her ear, on Wednesday evening.

"But she said she didn't mind that much because if you get a regular spot at the Momgambo someone from a record company might come and see you and then you'd get a dream come true."

"I think I'm dreaming now, Polly," Johnny said.

Polly smiled. And even though she couldn't see him, she knew he was smiling, too.

"Things have come right for Rod as well, Johnny."

Polly went on to tell him that news.

"But the best news, almost as good as Wilf coming to hear you play is..."

Polly glanced over her shoulder as someone tapped on the phone box door and then held up a hand to indicate she'd only be five minutes.

"I had a letter from Mum this morning," continued Polly. "Janice wrote and told her how we helped Anne on Sunday when she was lost. Janice must've sung your praises because Mum now thinks she might have been a bit hasty about things.

"She says as long as I don't go to any unsuitable places to watch you and the Skifflers... She even got the name right, and as long as I don't stay out too late, she doesn't mind me seeing you as long as I tell Gran where we're going. She said she's written to Gran as well. But I didn't have time to hear about that this morning.

"I opened my letter on the bus, and felt a right nitwit when I squealed out loud. But, I was that happy, Johnny."

"Me, too, Pippi. And I wish we were together now so I could show you how happy I am instead of just talking about it."

"We can't even talk any longer, Johnny. There's someone waiting to use the phone box. And she *doesn't* look happy about how long I'm keeping her waiting."

So, reluctantly, Polly said goodbye and went into the Momgambo to play Peggy Lee's *Johnny Guitar* on the jukebox because, same as in the song, there was never a man like her Johnny.

"And I'll be seeing my Johnny a week today," she told Kenneth. "And so will Wilf. Oh I do hope he'll like Johnny and the Skifflers."

Chapter Sixteen

The Man That Got Away
(Judy Garland)

"So you needn't have bothered trying to do a bit of match-making after all." Betty Jones laughed after Peggy told her about the letter from Ivy as they sat drinking tea in Betty's living room.

"To be fair, I gave that idea up once I saw how often Johnny was writing to our Polly and hearing that he phoned her at the phone box outside Jack's estate agent's shop every other night," said Peggy. "And that was before meeting him on Sunday."

"You liked him then?"

"He seems a right nice lad, Betty. I think Edna was right when she said it could be the real thing between him and Polly. But I'll be right glad not to feel I'm going against Ivy's wishes now. I'll even tell her when I write back that Johnny and his skiffling band will likely be playing at Jack and Edna's wedding reception."

"I hope they do, Peg. I'd love to hear them. Even though that record he made for your Polly was a bit crackly I thought Johnny's voice was lovely when she played it for us last night."

"Not surprised it sounded crackly, Betty. Our Polly must've played it a couple of dozen times since Sunday and it isn't made of the same stuff as records you buy in the shops."

Peggy nodded when Betty held the tea pot over her cup. She'd like a refill. One cup was never enough when having a good natter.

"You won't have to wait until the wedding reception to hear him and the lads, though, Betty. They're doing a couple of numbers at the Community Centre when we go to plan everything out for the reception. That was fixed so Jack and Edna could hear them before making up their minds. But now, someone even more important is coming to hear them as well."

"Blimey, Peg," Betty said when she'd heard what Polly had fixed up, "I wonder what this important chap's like? We won't have to get all dressed up because of him, will we?"

"I don't reckon he'll be interested in what two women our age are wearing, Betty. It'll be Johnny and maybe our Polly, too, getting his attention. She told me he said he never could resist a girl with red hair."

"And anyroads, Peg, you and me will be busy planning out how to decorate the place along with Rod and Jeff Simmonds. I still can't get over Rod having such a talent."

Peggy nodded. "It's right good Gilbert approves now and good Rod doesn't feel he has to keep what he does a secret from folk.

"Mind, Betty," she added. "You've got a talent when it comes to making shortbread biscuits. Do you think you could make a large batch of these for the reception?" she asked as she munched on another one of her friend's newly-baked biscuits. "They're delicious."

"I was going to offer to do just that, Peg. Thought I'd use the biscuit cutters my Mary gave me. Heart-shaped, they are so they'll look nice and romantic."

"And will taste like the food of love an' all," Peggy said. "We won't mention them in front of Edna, though. They can be a nice surprise for her on the day."

Peggy didn't like to think too much of the wedding day. Oh, she was happy for Edna, of course she was. But, even though Polly would still be around for a few weeks after the wedding, Peggy was sure she'd feel right lonely when Edna wasn't living with her any more.

"I'd best be going, Betty," she said, standing up and wiping the biscuit crumbs off her skirt. "It's almost time for *The Archers* and Edna's in so we can listen together. Must make the most of having her around while I can."

"Don't worry, Peg," Betty said, obviously guessing what her friend had been thinking, "I'm sure I won't be the only one who'll try and make sure you don't get too lonely when Edna's flown the nest."

Betty stood up, too, and Peggy knew her friend would walk to the gate with her and then they'd stand there chatting for a few more minutes.

"Thanks, Betty. "I keep telling myself I'll still have my friends," Peggy said as they went down the garden path. "And it isn't like Edna will be going miles away. It'll just take some getting used to it, that's all."

"Don't think about that yet, Peg." Betty opened the gate and when Peggy walked out, closed it and leant on the top bar. "Think of something else," she continued. "Like how this time next week we'll be at the Community Centre planning things, and we better make tick sheets before then to help us remember exactly what we want to work out and how to make them work out."

"I know how our Polly is hoping things will work out," said Peggy. "I don't suppose this time next week can get here quick enough for her."

"And here's Polly now, Peg, walking down the road with Gloria. It's nice they've become friends being near enough the same age as each other."

"Yes, Gloria was round at Maisie's last night when Polly went to pick out a pattern for her bridesmaid dress. Gloria's going with Polly to the Momgambo on Saturday to see the country and western duo perform," Peggy said.

"I reckon Polly wants to see if a live performance brings in a lot of people. If it does, I imagine this Wilf person will be anxious to have more of that sort of thing there so as long as he likes Johnny and the Skifflers..."

"Fingers crossed for next Wednesday then," said Betty.

*

"Crikey, Polly," Johnny said, glancing around the Community Centre as he and the Skifflers walked in carrying a washboard, a wash tub, a saw, a couple of jugs and a cigar box fiddle, "I thought it was just your gran, her friend and Edna and Jack who'd be here. Apart from your Wilf when he gets here of course. But..."

Polly smiled up at him, her heart fluttering as it always did when she looked into his eyes. "Dad had to go for a check-up so Mum booked them in for a couple of days at the hotel where she works so they could come and see you, though I'm sure they'll be seeing you at the reception on the day, too."

"And who are those two over by the far wall, Polly?"

"Rod and his brother. Measuring up for a mural that Rod's going to do for Jack and Edna. Rod still can't believe what good luck it was when his dad caught him doing the illustration for a cowboy comic which led to Mr Simmonds approving of him doing twee animal and fairy tale drawings, too. I bet there'll be animals and good luck fairies on the mural."

"Fingers crossed Rod's luck will rub off on me and Wilf will like what he hears tonight," said Johnny.

"No need for crossed fingers. I'm your lucky mascot, remember. Anyway, come and say hello to Jack and Edna and Gran and meet Gran's friend, Betty. Then you can have a word with Mum and be introduced to Dad."

Polly was so pleased to see the friendly way her dad spoke to Johnny. And her mum even told Johnny she was glad he hadn't let distance keep him away from Polly.

"And that," Polly said quietly to Johnny as they went back to the Skifflers, "is Mum's way of apologising for trying to split us up and letting you know she now accepts you as someone special to me."

"That's great, Pippi. I think me and the lads might just take a chance and do our version of *Yes, My Darling Daughter*, he added with a smile.

"I'll leave you to get organised," said Polly, glancing at her watch. "Wilf should be here any time now."

"Is that him, hovering in the doorway, Polly?"

Polly glanced over her shoulder and, as she met Wilf's gaze, he beckoned to her before stepping back outside.

Puzzled and slightly worried, Polly went out to join him.

He looked far from his usual serene self and Polly felt even more worried. Had he decided not to stay and hear Johnny after all?

"Is anything the matter, Wilf?" she asked.

"Which of the two older ladies is your grandma, Polly?"

The question surprised Polly and she hesitated before saying, "The one wearing the green jumper. But why… What…?"

"Just bear with me, Polly, I hope I'll get a chance to explain properly later. But for now, has she got anyone special, any man that is, in her life?"

"No, why?" Polly demanded, wondering if someone of Wilf's age could see someone across the room and fall in love.

"As I said, Polly, I hope to explain later. Now, do you reckon this Johnny of yours knows that song I like so much?"

"You mean the one you always play on the jukebox when you come to the Momgambo? But, that's called… Wilf, do you *know* my gran?"

"Never mind that now, Polly. Just go and ask Johnny if he and his band could play it. I'll come inside in a few minutes when... when, I've pulled myself together a bit."

*

"All right," Johnny said when Polly told him of Wilf's request. "We'll do *Wake the Town and Tell the People* for Jack and Edna, *Two Hearts, Two Kisses* for you, Pippi, the Mrs Brown song for your mum and then finish with the one Wilf wants which must be especially for your gran. I suppose love at first sight can hit at any age," he added.

"Wilf did look as if someone had hit him hard," said Polly. "His voice was a bit strange, too. Like it was coming from miles away."

Wilf came in a few minutes later and, Polly noticed, without looking around at anyone else, stood facing Johnny and the Skifflers.

Sounding slightly nervous, Johnny looked towards Jack and Edna, sitting on the edge of a long table with Polly's parents, and said their first number was especially for the happy couple.

Edna and Jack obviously loved the skiffle version of the song.

When the band played the Pat Boone song, everyone joined in the chorus.

"Bit of a cheeky one next, for my Polly's mum," said Johnny.

When that song was over and the laughter died down, Johnny said, "Now the last song is one that we haven't had much chance to rehearse but we've been asked to sing *Peg of My Heart* so here we go."

Polly saw Wilf turn to look towards her gran. She was standing close enough to her gran to see her clutch Betty's arm and to hear her gasp, "Oh, goodness, Betty. It's...it's my husband."

"Peg, love. It can't be. Your husband's name was Eddie and he died in the First World War."

Polly looked to where Edna was still sitting with Jack. Her mum and dad were still there, too. The four of them were chatting. They didn't look surprised or curious so they mustn't have noticed anything.

Her gran looked so shaky; Polly moved quickly to her other side.

Gran seemed unaware of Polly and said in a faint voice, "He was christened Wilfred but never used that version. Everyone called him Ed or Eddie and I never said he died, Betty, I said I lost him in the war. And I did. But now… Now…"

As the song came to an end, Polly saw her gran let go of Betty's arm and take a few faltering steps forward.

Looking towards Wilf, Polly watched as he walked towards her gran with his arms held wide.

"Could Peg be right, Polly?" Betty asked in an anxious-sounding whisper. "And if she is, what about Edna and your mum? I know Edna's always thought her dad died. But if this *is* Peg's husband, that means he's also…"

Polly looked over to the group sitting on the table and saw they'd become aware of something happening.

The sudden complete silence, as all eyes focussed on the grey-haired couple in the centre of the room was almost tangible.

Chapter Seventeen

A Fool Such as I
(Jo Stafford)

Out of the corner of her eye, Polly saw Rod and Jeff leaving. They'd obviously realised that whatever was happening it was a private matter.

Johnny clearly knew that, too, as walking round the edge of the room, he started to make his way over to Polly.

"I don't know what's going on there," he said, "but it looks like something much more important to Wilf than giving any decision right now about live performances at the Momgambo."

"Gran seems to think Wilf is Eddie, her husband," Polly whispered.

Johnny gave a low whistle. "Whichever way that turns out your gran will need you, Polly, and she won't want me and the others around. We'll grab our instruments and go. But we're not booked for tomorrow night so I'll leave work early and drive over and meet you in the Momgambo about half-five."

He gave her arm a loving squeeze and brushed his lips over her cheek before making his way back to the Skifflers.

Wilf glanced in Johnny's direction long enough to call, "You're hired," before looking down again at Polly's gran.

"Do you think I should go, too, Polly?" Betty asked once Johnny and the Skifflers had gone.

"You're gran's best friend, Betty. However this ends up, I think she'll need you. And I think maybe I should go over and tell Mum and Edna who Gran thinks Wilf is."

Polly took a few steps towards them but stopped when her gran moved slightly away from Wilf and spoke in a loud, but shaky voice.

"I've got a lot of explaining to do and I can't do it here, it'll have to be at home. So, Ivy, will you and Walter please come along with us, too?"

Polly could tell her gran wasn't too sure what the reply would be so she darted over to her parents. "Please, Mum," Polly said. "Please say you'll come."

Her mother pursed her lips and Polly looked at Edna perched on the other end of the table and sent a silent plea for help.

"Polly," said her aunt. "Do you know if Wilf is short for Wilfred?"

Edna had emphasised the last two letters of the name and Polly nodded.

"I think you should come with us, our Ivy," Edna said, leaning across Jack to look at her.

And seeing the expression on Edna's face, Polly thought maybe she'd guessed that it was possible Wilf might also be the father she and Ivy had thought was dead.

*

Half-an-hour later Peggy, sitting close to Wilf on the two-seater settee, looked around at the others as Betty handed out cups of tea.

Ivy, sitting in one of the armchairs, opposite Walter who looked tired, had a cold and hard look on her face. Peggy sighed.

She knew that the explaining she was about to do would either end in make or break between the two of them. Because as Peggy knew to her cost, her eldest daughter had discovered some of the truth long ago; but, to give Ivy her due, she'd never said a word to anyone else about it - except maybe Walter.

Betty, now with her own cup of tea, walked over to sit on one of the dining chairs brought over by Edna and Polly who'd placed two at one side of the settee and two at the other.

"This isn't only Peg's story, it's mine too, of course," said the man sitting next to Peggy. "Before the war, the first one, I mean, I was always know to Peg and others as Ed or Eddie. I became Wilf during that war because there were too many other soldiers alongside me called Ed, Ted and Fred."

"Even if Polly had referred to you as Ed or Eddie, I'd never in a month of Sundays imagined you were Eddie my husband," Peggy told him. "Though I knew you must still be alive. My heart would've told me if you weren't."

"I don't know what that's got to do with Edna and me always being told you *were* dead," Ivy said. "Even though I eventually–"

"I never said that, Ivy. I always said we'd lost him in the war. And I know that implied the other thing but there was, I thought at the time, a good reason for me explaining to you why he hadn't come home after the war."

"I'll tell them how that came about, Peg. After all, it was *my* fault you had to say why I wasn't back with you.

"I came home on leave in the January of 1918 and had a couple of weeks with Peg before returning to fight," he said, glancing at Edna. "It wasn't long before I got myself knocked up a bit and, eventually, ended up in a convalescence home in Cheshire. That was in the March, I think."

"It was." Peggy nodded. "I don't know if you remember going to stay with your grandparents, Ivy, my parents who both died before the second war. You were coming up to six at the time."

"I remember," said Ivy. "But me going to stay there doesn't explain things, either."

"It does in a way, Ivy, because you went there so I could go and stay near where Eddie was and go and visit him every day. But–"

"But I was a broken man, Ivy, in body and in mind. I told your mum we had no chance of being together again. I wasn't going to put her through the hell I was going through. Nightmares, screaming, lashing out physically at anyone who dared touch me."

He reached out for his cup of tea and drained it before continuing. "Your mum begged and pleaded, said she'd take care of me, make me whole again. But I wouldn't listen. There's a song about a fool such as I," he added.

Peggy smiled and nodded, understanding her Eddie was trying to lighten the tense atmosphere a bit. "Go on, Eddie," she said.

"Well, one day I just walked out of the convalescent home and made my way, god only knows how, to an army mate's house in London.

Without even knowing Peg was expecting another baby," he added, looking at Edna again.

"I hadn't clicked on to that myself then," Peggy told them, glad to see Jack comforting Edna who was understandably emotional.

"I thought being sick and all that was down to nerves and worry," she continued. "And even though he disappeared, Ivy, he paid money into my bank account for you and me through a solicitor regular as clockwork, though I never could find out *where* he was."

Betty got up and took the teapot into the kitchen. Peggy silently blessed her friend for being there and seeing they all had much needed cups of tea.

"So why didn't *you* tell me the truth when I found out some of it for myself?" Ivy demanded.

Peggy watched her daughter's gaze turn onto Eddie.

"I found out you weren't dead just after my twenty-first birthday," Ivy told him. "I tracked your mum, my grandmother down, went to visit her without Mum knowing. She, your mother, told me you weren't dead but Mum had turned you out. But she wouldn't tell me where you were."

"I'll have a few words to say to Ma about that," said Eddie.

"No, Eddie, love. It's water under the bridge and your mother must be old and frail now. Besides, she likely only said that because she needed to believe it herself."

Peggy looked back at Ivy. "And when you challenged me about him still being alive, Ivy, I did admit he wasn't dead just that I'd implied that."

"I still want to know why you let us think otherwise in the first place. It was cruel, Mum, really, really cruel."

All eyes were on her now and Peggy felt a nauseating sinking of despair. They all looked as if they agreed with Ivy. Except maybe Betty and, and…

Peggy looked up as Polly came and sat on the arm of the settee and put an arm around her shoulders. "I'm sure you had a good reason, Gran."

Then Polly glanced across at her mother. "If you stop going on about it, Mum, it will give Gran a proper chance to tell you."

"Polly," began her mother, "I will not have you–"

But Polly's father interrupted in a quiet but firm voice. "Polly's right, Ivy. Let Peggy explain."

Surprised but grateful for her son-in-law's verbal support, Peggy took a deep breath.

"If it had been known your dad had left us," she said, "you'd have got picked on at school and called after in the street. Young children call others awful names, say unkind things without realising the harm and hurt it can cause."

"Gran's right about that, Mum," said Polly. "Can't you remember how many times I came home from school upset because I'd been called Ginger or Carrots or Freckle-face? If you'd been called names because your daddy had left you, it would have been awful."

"I didn't want any of that sort of thing for you, Ivy," said Peggy. "It seemed best to let everyone think what I let you, and later you, Edna, think."

"Actually," said Ivy, "I do remember when I was

about eleven getting in a fight with a boy in my class and he said I couldn't even get my dad to stick up for me because my dad was dead."

"Does that mean you can understand why Gran let you think he was?" said Polly.

"You should do, Ivy," said Edna. "Because you've done and said things because of being worried by what others might say. And if I can understand and forgive Mum for letting me believe my father died before I was born, you should be able to as well."

"I don't know how you work that out, Edna. But, yes, I am beginning to understand and maybe in time, I'll forgive as well. Now, though, Walter looks worn out. Where's the nearest phone box so I can phone for a taxi to get us back to the hotel."

"No need for that, Edna. I'll take you in the car."

Peggy's heart sank as Eddie stood up. She'd only just found him after all these years and, although she knew he wouldn't disappear out of her life, she wanted him to stay here a bit longer now.

"You come, too, Peg," Eddie said. "We can have a good long talk on the way back. But first..."

He walked over to Edna. "I'm right sorry I didn't know I had two daughters, lass. I'm not saying it would have been any different if your mum had realised she was expecting again and told me so. But I hope you and Ivy will let me get to know the two of you now. Better late than never."

"You've found me in time to give me away," said Edna. "I'm sure Donald will understand I want my father and not my godfather to do that, Mum?" she added looking at Peggy.

"'Course he will, love. "Me and the girls lived next door to Donald and his wife Mavis when we moved to Salford soon after Edna was born," she told Eddie.

"I was still hoping I might be able to find you, Eddie, so I waited a while until I had Edna christened. By that time, Mavis and Donald had become right good friends so I asked them to be Edna's godparents.

"We moved here six years back, Mavis and Donald moved from Salford as well, went to live in Bolton. We've only seen each other once in a blue moon since but we've always kept in regular touch."

"Peg," said Eddie. "Your, no, *our* son-in-law looks dead on his feet. Let's get going."

Peggy nodded and watched Polly walk over to Ivy, watched Ivy and Walter return Polly's hug and heard Ivy say, "We're going back to Wales, Friday morning, Polly. But we'll be home for the wedding and I'm sure we'll be writing to each other a lot before then. And your Johnny's got a lovely voice, love, even when he makes it all skiffle-like."

"I'll wash up these cups and saucers then get off home, Peg," Betty told her. "Pop round tomorrow *if* you've time. I'm right glad for you, love," she added, wiping a tear away before glancing at Eddie. "I'm sure I'll be seeing you again," she told him.

"And I guess you'll be coming in when you bring Gran home, so I'll see you then, Wilf, or should I call you Eddie now?" said Polly.

Peggy hid a smile. There was one thing Polly hadn't quite realised yet. "Think about that one while we're gone, Polly," she said.

Chapter Eighteen

Music! Music! Music!
(Teresa Brewer)

"For heaven's sake, Polly," said Kenneth. "The noise of you stirring that coffee, that doesn't even need stirring, is hurting my ears. Why don't you play a song on the jukebox while you're waiting for your Johnny to get here? We don't want to have it all quiet and gloomy when others start coming in, either."

It was half-past five and Polly was longing for Johnny to arrive. She couldn't wait to tell him everything that had happened after he and the Skifflers had left the Community Centre last night. Nor to see his face when other things happened, she thought.

"Right, I'll do it," Kenneth said.

He came from behind the counter and put a coin in the slot.

Polly had to smile when the sound of *Music! Music! Music!* filled the place.

"Good song that is," said Johnny walking in and smiling at Polly. "*"All I want is kissing you"*," he said, joining in with Teresa Brewer's song, after giving Polly a quick kiss.

"You been here long?" he asked when he'd stopped singing.

"Not really. It felt like hours waiting for you, though. I got here early. Jack brought me in the car. He gave me today off work. He's gone to...to see Edna now."

Heck, she'd nearly let it slip that Jack had gone to fetch Edna. To bring her here along with…

"So, come on, Pippi. Tell me how it all finished up. "*Is* Wilf your gran's husband?"

Polly nodded. "And it took ages for it to dawn how that makes him my grandad," she said, laughing. "But that happened after he'd taken Mum and Dad back to their hotel."

Kenneth brought two coffees over and, after thanking him, Polly shook her head. "I've started at the wrong end of it, Johnny. You know that song about a dream walking? Well, Gran's been like that since last night when you played *Peg of My Heart*.

"I feel like I'm in a bit of a dream and I know Edna does as well. Not sure about Mum but I think she'll get on better with Gran now she's heard what happened. Gran and Wilf have gone to see them at the hotel because Dad was too tired to stay at Gran's too long last night."

"I suppose you'll get to the beginning in the end, Pippi."

Polly's heart leaped as she saw the amused but loving look in Johnny's eyes.

"Right," she said and went on to tell him her gran and grandad's sad story.

"But it's got a happy ending, Johnny. He's coming back to Gran. She never stopped loving him, and he never stopped loving her. That's why neither of them ever put in for a divorce. Fancy, they're still married after being apart thirty-seven years."

"Right true love, that is, Pippi."

Polly nodded.

"And Edna never got to tell you but of course she wants you to play at the wedding reception. Oh, and Wilf, I mean Grandad, will be giving her away at the wedding. And Mum said you've got a lovely voice." She glanced out of the window and smiled to see two cars pulling up. Jack's and her grandad's.

And she laughed when the passengers and drivers got out.

"We're having a celebratory party, Johnny," she told him as her gran and new-found grandad, Betty, Jack and Edna and Rod Simmonds walked in.

"It isn't only to celebrate Gran and Grandad's reunion," she said. "There's something else as well. But Grandad and Rod will explain that bit," she added, laughing again as her grandad walked over to the jukebox and selected his favourite song.

"Coffees all round, coming up, Wilf," Kenneth called as everyone sat down.

"You can call me that as well, Johnny," said Polly's grandad. "Wilfred's the name I'll be writing on our agreement, if you agree of course."

"I've not told him anything about that," Polly said.

She glanced out of the window again. There was still one more car to come if what she'd tried to arrange worked out.

"Don't tell him yet, Grandad. I think you know who have just arrived," she said.

"Your mum and dad, Polly?" Johnny asked.

"They can't come, Johnny," said her gran. "We did ask them but Polly's dad is still a bit tired and they've got a train journey back to Wales tomorrow. Eddie offered to drive them there but Ivy can't take a long journey in cars or buses.

"But they both seemed happy enough about everything when Eddie and I left them so we could get here on time."

"Then who?" Johnny looked puzzled and Polly smiled.

She giggled as Johnny's expression changed to one of utter astonishment as his parents, his uncle, whose cellar the band used for rehearsals, and the Skifflers came in.

"I sent a telegram to your mum," Polly explained, "and asked her to try and get everybody here and not to let you know anything if you happened to go home before coming here."

After some rather muddled introductions all round, Polly said, "And now, my grandad, Wilf, has something to say and after that, Rod has something to show."

"Thank you, Polly," her grandad said, grinning at her before turning to Johnny. "Right, lad, I vaguely recall telling you last night you were hired. But I didn't mean for just one live performance.

"I'd like to book Johnny Jake and the Skifflers to play here at the Momgambo once a week, same night every week so folk will get to know when to come and hear you. That can be sorted when you work out what nights any other bookings are for.

"Polly told me you'll be at the Hippodrome for a full week soon, so we'll have to allow for that when you sign the agreement. That's if you want to of course. Even though you're Polly's boyfriend we need it on a proper business footing."

Stella, Johnny's mum, squealed in delight and got

up to throw her arms around Johnny. "I'm that proud of you, son," she said, and Johnny's dad agreed in a gruff voice.

"Knew it was a good idea for you lot to rehearse in my cellar," Johnny's uncle said. "It might be a famous place when you make it big time, Johnny."

"If I could get a word in here," said Johnny, his eyes shining and a huge grin on his face, "I know I'm speaking for the Skifflers as well when I say we'll be delighted to sign the agreement, Wilf."

"Of course you will," Polly said. "I never had any doubt. That's why when I saw Rod in his garden at lunch time, he was on a day off as well, I asked him do something special."

She nudged Rod. "Go on, show him," she ordered.

Rod reached inside his leather jacket and pulled out a roll of paper. Smiling, he unrolled it to show Johnny.

It was a poster with a life-like painting of Johnny and the Skifflers and their instruments.

"It needs words adding to it," Rod said. "Johnny Jake and the Skifflers appearing live at the Momgambo every Thursday. Or whatever night you decide on."

"Rod, this is great, really great," said Johnny. "Thank you."

"I think it's you we should all be thanking, Polly, love," said her gran. "Without you, none of any of this would have happened. Eddie and me would never have met again, Edna and your mum would never have got to know their dad, Edna and Jack wouldn't have had an about to be famous band playing at their reception and–"

"I wouldn't have got the extra commissions for illustrating," interrupted Rod.

"Stop it," Polly protested, feeling her face burning. "Really, it's Mum we should be thanking. If she hadn't packed me off to stay with you, Gran…"

"An ill wind that blew good," her gran said, teasingly.

"Right, so now things are mostly sorted," said Polly, looking at the Skifflers.

"Did you bring your skiffle instruments like I put in the telegram to Stella?"

"In Johnny's uncle's van outside," Graham said, grinning.

"So, go and fetch them," said Polly. "You can play all the right sort of songs to celebrate everybody's good luck."

Polly smiled when her grandad said, "As long as the first of Johnny Jake and the Skifflers' live performances here at the Momgambo starts and ends with the song that's number twelve on the jukebox. Because Polly told Peg how I play that song every time I come here. In case you haven't worked out what it is yet, it's…"

"*Peg of My Heart*," chorused those who knew it was a special song.

And ten minutes later when Johnny and his Skifflers performed that song, Polly wondered if anyone else noticed how, right near the end of it, Johnny looked at her and changed the name Peg to Polly:

"I love you, Polly of my heart…"

THE END

Acknowledgements

And the Jukebox Played their Song started life as a People's Friend Pocket Novel under the title A Song on the Jukebox and was also published by Linford Romance Large Print.

Thank you to David Young for the cover illustration.

Thanks to all the readers who told me Broome Park Prefab Village stories brought back happy memories and asked for a long story about the village and the characters.

And a special thank you to Jo Bartlett.

41846371R00096

Printed in Poland
by Amazon Fulfillment
Poland Sp. z o.o., Wrocław